A League of My Own

Like Mother, Like Daughter

A Novel by

JT Terry

Perfectly Brown

An Imprint of Perfectly Brown, LLC
Perfectlybrown.com
Cover design by Jobyna Terry
Copyright © 2023 Jobyna Terry
Published by Kindle Direct Publishing
ISBN 9781736932414 (Paperback Edition)

Revolution is a serious thing, the most serious thing about a revolutionary life. When one commits oneself to the struggle, it must be for a lifetime.
- Angela Davis

TABLE OF CONTENTS

ANGELA SUTTON

I sat there in the dark waiting for his arrival. I attach my silencer and turn on my laser. My gun was cocked and loaded. Time always seems to move slow when you're in the midst of a mission. Not knowing if everything you planned will go perfectly. Constantly running Plan A and Plan B through your mind. In just seconds your body goes into adrenaline mode when you see lights coming down a driveway or hear a key opening a door.

General Christop Conrad is my second hit of tonight and if time is on my side no one has discovered General Boris Igor. As soon as I hear him unlocking the door, I aim my laser right where his head should be. This should be an easy kill, but I need to know where he has the files stored first. When he looks up from the doorknob, he notices the laser beam between his eyes.

"Hello General, please walk towards the laser."

"Wer bist du?"

"Now, now, General. We both know you speak English very well. Please engage me properly."

"Who are you and what is the meaning of this?"

"You have some very important information that we need."

"Who is we?"

"Does code name 'Hidden Darkness' ring a bell?"

"Listen, I don't want any trouble. I have nothing here at my home."

I step closer to him with my gun still aiming at his head.

"Give me the files and speak nothing of this and I will spare your life."

"My wife and daughter will be here soon. Can you please give me a chance."

"Where are the files?"

"They're on my computer. My computer on our base."

"Here, write down the building and office location."

He began to write the information down. The same man who thought that he could secretly enslave a village in Benin to manufacture weapons is the same man about to beg for his life. Typical.

"Thank you for this information. Let's shake on it."

He reaches for my hand to shake. Little does he know, it's laced with a poison that if it encounters your skin, it will make your heart stop in 15 minutes.

"Well General, I see your family is arriving. Try to have a better night."

"Thank you. Thank you", He said breathing shakily.

I walk backwards toward the rear door, and he watches me take every step. Then he looks to see his family approaching the front door. I slip out of the back and take the glove off then place it into a plastic bag. I run to the woods and grab the motorcycle I came over on, then push it to the road.

After I make it to the road, I start it and head to the base. I toss the poison glove alongside the road. When I am about a half of a mile away, I look at the base's map then abandon the bike. I run the rest of the way. I make it onto the base and to the designated building, undetected.

Ch-Chick.

I cock my pistol and quickly sneak down the shadows of the hall so no one or cameras can detect my presence. There could be a trap anywhere, so I chose my next steps carefully with every deep breath. Finally, I arrive to the general's office. I know I must get in and out. I pull out my trip wire and unlock the door. I shine my flashlight around the room to see if there are any traps then proceed to sit at the desktop.
Damn. It's locked.

I start the computer in safe mode so I can hack into the system without a passcode. As soon as I stick my flash drive in to begin the extraction, sirens began blaring.

BEEP! BEEP! BEEP! Eindringlingsalarm!

BEEP! BEEP! BEEP! Eindringlingsalarm!

I hear agents running and shouting everywhere and I need to find a way out of here. I have at least 30 seconds before the extraction finishes downloading onto the flash drive, and I can hear them screaming commands in German as they run down the hall. They are inching closer to me by the second. *Shit*! This is taking forever, and I can feel my heart beating in my throat. The door begins to open, and I know I have to make myself invisible, so I snatch the flash drive out of the computer and hide behind the curtains with the darkest shadows. Sweat beads roll down the sides of my lips.

I see the flashlights and red dots scanning the room as I try to hold my breath, so they don't hear me. "Der Eindringling ist nicht da!", yells one of their soldiers over the walkie and the others run out of the room. Once I know they haven't seen me, I take a deep breath then open the window and secure my grappling hook. I scan the area to make sure that there are no soldiers near the brush I intend to land in. I kiss my ankh and climb out of the window then scale down the side of the building. Finally, on the ground, I look around and make a run for it. I have been treading a real fine line between my missions for The League and the Marines.

I make it out of the woods and to the main street right in time to flag a taxi. I sit in the back of the taxi out of breath and sweaty. Luckily, I make it back to my barracks in time to report for curfew. Lord knows I need a good night's rest. Two assassinations in one night, sheesh. I have to do what I have to do. Those German officials had to go down before they outed our other

League assassins for the American Embassy hit. My body was aching, it felt like I had midgets dancing on my body with cleats on. I am going out to get a drink tomorrow. I close my eyes hoping for a decent night of sleep without the nightmares or racing thoughts.

[The Marine Hymn begins to play] Morning always comes in a hurry and nighttime always seems to escape me. I'm not on duty for either organization tonight so it is time to get out and see some sights.

"Hey Morales, are you up?"

"Ay, dios mío! Sutton, you always do this! Girl, I am trying to sleep in today."

"We are a long way away from home and there is plenty to see, we might as well enjoy it."

Morales rolls her eyes, but she knows we know how to turn a city out. We get dressed and head out to the nearest bar. Morales and I have been connected at the hip since we enlisted in the Marines. She was Cuban and Jamaican, originally from the Bronx. Morales was probably one of the most beautiful women I had ever seen other than myself. I know people always asked why in the hell are we Marines.

Morales has a pixie cut, milk chocolate skin, honey-colored eyes, and stood about 5'8 with a slender frame. She probably weighed 130 soaking wet. She was an only child, so she welcomed our sisterhood with open arms. Sis could burn too, my lord. The struggle didn't seem so rough as long as we were on tour together.

"Where the hell are we Sutton? Mami you cannot keep bringing us to every hole in the wall."

"Some local pub, word around the barracks is they make the strongest drinks."

As we walk up to the bar, I see this fine brother standing there. He is the best-looking thing I have seen in a long time. He must be about 6'3, 6'4. He looks like he may play football with those broad shoulders and big hands. He has a nice butt too and dark how I like my coffee. Clean shaved with a mustache. Succulent lips. MMM mmmm! I want to see how he's going to act with me playing hard to get. I walk over and stand next to him at the bar. Damn, he smells good too.

"Excuse me miss, can I..."

"No, you cannot, I don't accept drinks from strangers. Thank you."

"Well, Miss..." he looks at my name tag, "Sutton, I was only going to ask for you to pass me that menu behind you."

I wasn't embarrassed at all, hell my plan had worked.

"I apologize, here you are," then proceeded to hand him the menu.

"My name is Brian, and it's a pleasure to meet you, Miss Sutton. Thank you for all your hard work and be safe out there." I nod with a smile, and he walks away to go sit at a table.

"ANG! Mi dead wid laugh when he checked you."

"Child, that was a part of my plan. They like when you play hard to get."

"I like my men easy. You know the kind...they like to kick up rumpus!"

"Bazodee lady, eh?"

We laugh and go on to explore the rest of the town. I loved boxing and I heard there would be a match later.

We figure there would be some hot men at the match, so we change out of uniform and dressed in our best civilian clothing. I love showing off my legs, so a dress and some cute heels were my only choice.

I had no idea that I would see that fine man from the bar again at the boxing match. I think he said his name is Brian. I didn't know what to expect but it turned out to be great match honestly. He went up against Felix Hans, a German Heavy Weight Champion, who stood 6'7, weighing 225 pounds. But, Brian kicked his ass in 3 rounds with a K.O. He was a damn good boxer and boxing is my favorite sport. I love the technique and skill of it.

It was so exciting to see him fight, it was almost like he was fighting for my honor once he saw I was in the crowd. We made eye contact every time he sat down. After the constant eye contact, I knew I had to make a move on this man before I truly never saw him again. That would be a pity because we had an instant connection.

Once his fight was over, I made my way over to the boxing ring. I made sure to give him a proper hello and my number.

"Hi, I'm Angela. Congratulations on your win."

"Hi, I'm Brian and I'm a sag. Thank you, Ms. Angela Sutton."

We laugh and I kiss him on the lips. He kisses me back and it felt so different. Like leg pop different. I didn't think he would be as excited about me as I was about him. His team sweep him out of the ring, and I waited for him. He came out of the locker room with a huge smile and his duffle bag. Morales had left with one of the other Marines we knew, so I knew she was fine.

"So, what's next?"

"You tell me, I don't have anything planned." He reaches over and grabs my hand.

"I've always wanted to walk down Romantic Road. Want to join me?"

I nod with a smile, and he leads the way. It was the weekend, so I didn't have a curfew to keep. We spent all night walking and talking. He invited me to his hotel for a nap since he would be leaving in a few hours. I questioned what would happen after the most amazing night of my life. When I woke up, he was there lying next to me and had been watching me sleep.

"I want to keep seeing you, Angela. No matter what it takes."

"I want to keep seeing you too B!"

"B huh? I have a nickname already. Must be true love."

"Only time will tell huh?"

We share a kiss and agree to make us work no matter how hard it may be. By the time I knew what was happening, between the Marines, The League, and Love, I was spinning. Although some days were harder than others, Brian always brought balance to my life. His love was unconditional.

He knew it was more to my life than I could talk about at times, and he accepted it out of his love for me. What more could I ask for? I knew one day I would have to let him in. I couldn't lead him blindly into my life. He was patient with me, and I was grateful.

LIGHTS OUT

I am close to building up enough information to bury the U.S. government for its part in violating the basic human rights of black and brown people. The constitution means absolutely nothing to the machine that allows this country to dehumanize a race of people. Once all of this is out in the open, my people will finally get the relief and rights they deserve. NATO and the other global leaders will no longer be able to ignore it.

Shit, I'm not even sure who I can trust outside of Mama, especially with this type of information. I think I better give her my black book before I go out in the field tomorrow. If I keep pacing the floor like this, Brian is surely going to wake up. My anxiety has been through the roof these last few days. It's never good when I get this way because it messes with my focus. I grab my phone and text my girls to let them know I love them.

I think I should go sit with the ancestors before I go to bed. I need to get some clarity and talking to them always soothes my spirit. I walk into the family room and sit near the ancestral altar. I look up at Poppy, the start of this lifestyle we live now. I stare at his photo and smile. Such a patient and loving man, but he would slit an enemy's throat with no remorse when it came to his family, especially Nanny, my grandmother.

Poppy taught me so much before he passed away. Mostly never trust anyone you work for because they could switch on you just as fast as the enemies, they have you pursue. Poppy ultimately left The League because they stopped seeing eye to eye for what was best for Barbados and Nanny's health was starting to deteriorate.

Since mama was already involved with the League when Poppy was coming out, no one batted an eye and the legacy continued. When she met my Daddy, they were kind of like Velcro. They grew up together in Bridgetown. Eventually, they both were in The League, kicking ass and taking names. That was until she got pregnant with Avery. Daddy elected to be a stay-at-home dad and The League was fine with it because they couldn't control his wild behind. The only person he would listen to is mama.

They moved to the U.S. shortly before Avery was born so we could be citizens. I wish he would come to visit more but all he says is, "My pickney, ye know me hate the America. That's why I stay home until your mama fusses at me to come visit. Whitey is too entitled for me blood. Corrupt they are. Keep me grandbabies and ya mama safe, girl."

Out of all my siblings, Jack takes after Daddy the most. Stubborn, wild, hot-tempered, and loud, but will always be there when you need him. My right-hand man. He probably should've been my twin. We're 10 months apart. I love my family. I sat in front of the altar and meditated until I felt a soft kiss on my forehead. It was my baby coming to check on me because I hadn't gotten into bed yet.

"Are you alright sweet cheeks?"

"A little anxious about tomorrow. It's a solo assignment and you know I normally have Max to watch my back."

"Aww baby, you have trained all your life to watch your own back if you need to. You'll be fine. Now come to bed so your man can help you with some of that anxiety."

"Now honey don't threaten me with a good time."

"Baby it's not a threat it's a promise. Now come on get up out of that floor."

He lifts me off the floor and carries me to the bedroom. He lays me down on the bed and grabs his massage oils to rub me down. Before he could even finish the massage, I was knocked out.

It was the morning of Good Friday, I could smell the breakfast cooking and my girls laughing. Soli had come home from Bowie State and Shunny must've come home early from her sleepover when she smelled her Daddy's cooking. I got up and put my suit on then went downstairs. Home. This was the safest place on earth for me.

"Well, hello my loves!"

"Hey Ma! I figured I would pop in since today is a big day for you." My baby Soli came over to hug me.

"A big day for me?"

"Yea Pops said you're going on a solo assignment today."

"Yeaaaaaa", I had to scoff because I was not excited about today. I still had a gut feeling something was off but after praying to the ancestors, I left my faith and protection in their hands. As anxious as I was, I couldn't show any fear. I've always taught my girls that faith wards off fear, so I had to believe that to be true. As I sat down for breakfast, my work phone began ringing.

"Hello? Yes, this is Waytes. Sure, I can get there a little earlier. Thanks"

"Who was that baby?" Brian looks at me concerned.

"Nelson Fuentes"

"Big boss?"

"Yea, big boss. Not sure what the hell he wants but he can wait. I'll be there when I get there." My gut never lied. Every time I was around that man my skin crawled. The stack of files I had on him, and his corrupt shit made my blood boil. He was going to be my first target. "Ang, eat your food," Brian caught me in thought, but I began to eat my breakfast.

"Thanks for breakfast guys, I love yall."

"Love you too!" they all say together. I gather my stuff and Brian walks me to the car.

"Baby, you call me if anything goes down or you don't feel safe. Do you understand me?"

"Yes love. I love you. Take care of our girls."

"No doubt about that honey. I love you."

We kiss and I get into the car to head to the office. On the way, I stop at mama's house. I needed to feel her embrace and receive knowledge before I went into this place against my gut. I park in the backyard and walk in the back door.

"Mommmmm!"

"Angie is that you?"

"Yea, I wanted to talk to you before I went to work today. I've been having a bad feeling."

"What have you been feeling?"

"Just a bunch of anxiety, my chest has been feeling tight, a ton of sweating."

"Come on baby, let's go pull Sara. Our ancestors will never leave you unprotected or unguided." We walk over to her altar, and she began to pour libations and pray over me. She squeezes my hand, and I felt a warmness over my body.

"My Dearheart, I love you. Be ready. Today will change your life but you will be ok."

"Thanks, Mom. Here, I need you to take this book and this flash drive. It's everything I have found so far. Take care of it and my babies. If something happens to me. Give it to Solice and Shunny when the time is right."

"I will always take care of my family. You call me if you need me to frig 'em up. I'll be there like split splat." She shakes her fist in the air.

"Yes, I love you. I'll see you later."
I left out of the house and continued to work. When I arrived at the office, I met Max outside. She hated Fuentes just as much as I did.

"Did you hear?"

"Hear what?"

"I've been summoned by Fuentes."

"What? Why? Where's Laskins?"

"Who knows where that coward is? Any time Fuentes is contacting me directly, I know there is some bullshit involved. Watch and see."

She nods at me, and we bump fists. We walk through the doors and head up to our floor. I head to Fuentes office and knock on the door.

"Yes, sir."

"Ah, Good Morning Waytes, have a seat. Thank you for joining me a little earlier today. I want to make sure I could brief you on your new assignment since Laskins is out on leave for a couple of weeks."

"Laskins is on leave?" Laskins seldom takes a vacation and certainly not for long periods.

"Yes, he has some personal things going on."

"Okay, So this assignment. Tell me about it."

"We need you working on internal moles. This was your specialty in the Marines, and I want to use your expertise in finding out who has been tapping into several governmental agencies' databases."

My stomach drops because why in the world would he want me on this assignment unless he knew it was me and The League accessing the databases.

"Okay, is there a file?"

"Yes, here. Also, I have set up a meeting with one of my top cybersecurity specialists. He's about 30 minutes from here. Additionally, your normal vehicle is being serviced today. Please take this instead." He tosses me some keys and the file. I walk out of his office and look over at Morales and twitched my nose. She knew that meant being on the lookout for some bull today.

I walk to the parking lot and find the SUV he switched me to. I turn my League tracker on and get in the truck to head to the cyber security specialist's location in Kent Island, Maryland. Why in the hell would they have a specialist out there? I text Morales the location I was going to for safety measures. I pull out of the parking lot and begin driving. After about 15 minutes into the drive, I notice someone tailing me. I knew the bridge was coming up, so I was hoping to lose them. As soon as I sped up, they sped up. When I switched lanes, they switched lanes.

Shit. Shit. Shit. I can't endanger these people's lives who are driving around me. I cut to a country road after the bridge, and they still manage to locate me. I mash the gas and look for places to lose them. I knew I had to get out of this truck. This is probably how they're tracking me. This was a setup! Fucking Fuentes! I bash the GPS out on the dash and pull at some of the wires under the steering wheel. I get down the road and there's a truck blocking the road. I throw the truck in reverse and back up.

The other truck is still making its way behind me. I turn down an embankment and try to get away from them. As I try to press the brakes, they stop working and I'm going too fast to jump out. This can't be the end. The truck barrels over a cliff and I'm headed down towards the river. The doors wouldn't unlock and before I could do anything else, it was lights out.

7 YEARS

Here, we are again, celebrating the life of my mother, my super-shero, my heart. They claim time makes the loss easier, but the last 7 years haven't gotten any easier for me. Everything was going well and just like that she was gone. Just reflecting on the weeks leading up to her death, nothing makes sense. It was almost as if she knew something was going down.

It was like she started nesting and preparing for it. She and Pops made sure their wills were done, they moved properties in my and Shunny's names, they took out life insurance policies on one another, and she created a trust fund for us. Someone is behind her death and I'm going to find out who it is.

The day before it happened, there she was in the garden, smiling from ear to ear, with that gap that we picked on her about, her curls blowing in the wind, and her beautiful brown skin glowing in the afternoon sun. I remember walking in the backyard yelling. "Hey, Shorty!

Be careful out there, you know all your plants are taller than you, and you might get lost."

She was only 5'5 but reminded you of Pam Grier in her younger days, especially with the fire and sass. "Haha, very funny Solice, come on over here and help your mama pick this squash." She loved that damn garden, you might as well call her Jody's mama instead of Solice's and Oshun's mama.

I remember our last talk.

***

"Oh Soli, if only we had more time on this Earth, we could get so much done. We could change so many lives. Especially the lives of our people, you know?"

"Ma you're only 56, you act like you're going to be gone tomorrow, you have plenty of time to finish what we've started."

"That's just it, Soli, tomorrow isn't promised, baby. You do what you can and pass the torch and information to the younger generation. You and your sister have everything you need. Your Daddy and I have prepared you girls to take over when it's time."

"Lady, what are you talking about? Shunny is almost done with high school, she's not ready to take over and Pops has me running all over the globe with wine shows. I....", she raised her fingers to my lips to stop me. "Solice, you both are my daughters, and the granddaughters of Jean Sutton, my love, you all are prepared for what is up ahead. Use everything, E-V-E-R-Y-T-H-I-N-G, we have shown and given to you. Do you understand?" I looked into her dark brown eyes, and I felt no fear, but I felt uneasy. After locking eyes with her, I quickly glanced away to see Pops and Shad smiling at us from the kitchen window.

The next day, she was called on an assignment for the FBI. It was the morning of Good Friday and I had to head back to campus after breakfast. I kissed her and Pops on the forehead. She seemed okay, not exactly her usual self but okay. She was distracted after she got that phone call. Most of the time she didn't travel alone, but this time it was different. They sent her partner, Maxine Morales, who we call Aunty Max, on a separate assignment.

While driving to the site, "reports" claim that she lost control of her vehicle, which flipped several times and landed in a nearby river. They recovered the vehicle, but not Mom. Even after all these years, she was never recovered, and we have had to live with that. The fact that her agency nor The League could not find her, or an actual cause of death never sat well with me.

This wouldn't be the first time they covered a murder up. At this point, I don't know if my mother is dead or alive, but what I do know is I'm going to uncover whatever she was working on that would make someone want to have her killed. Starting with her boss Nelson and everyone in his circle. For the last 7 years, I have been sorting out my mother's "other" life, while my life began to fall apart.

I guess I thought I could protect Shad, my now ex-husband, like my mother protected Pops, but "Don't ask, don't tell," didn't work in our household. Unfortunately, he was a man who knew his wife and noticed when I started to change. I never really wanted to become an assassin, but I guess like mother, like daughter. Someone must carry on her legacy.

Looking back, I definitely would've wanted a normal life. Although Pops didn't know all the details about everything she was into and didn't care to know, Angela, the trained assassin, made sure her daughters knew who and what their mother was. There weren't many of us in the world, but she would always say, "We're in a league of our own. We're hidden in plain sight, but one mistake as an assassin could end your life." So that led me to wonder, did she make a mistake while working across enemy lines? Should she have gotten out sooner?

Why didn't the league protect her? Did she know that what she was doing would get her killed? I turn my attention back to Pops as he starts his speech, "Here's, to my beautiful Angela, my world, the mother of my two beautiful daughters, Solice and Oshun, my business partner, retired Marine Officer, and bad-ass FBI agent. She was so much more than this, so much more than words could ever describe. I miss you dearly my sweet." He smiles as he raises his glass in the air with a tear in the corner of his eye. Mom tried her best to shield him from her reality, but Pops wasn't dumb by a long shot. He just understood the assignment of "Don't ask, don't tell."

He knew for some stuff, it was better that he didn't know what she was up to, but Mom knew, whenever she needed her knight in shining bulletproof vest, Pops was down to ride. Don't get twisted, Pops was pretty bad-ass himself. He kind of gives off a Delroy Lindo vibe or at least that's who people say he looks like. He was not only a successful international wine business owner, but he was an Olympic boxer, skilled in Muay Thai, and a black belt in Taekwondo, which I help him teach every other weekend.

He seems "okay" but that tear in his eye told me everything I needed to know. Pops was hurting but trying to continue to celebrate the love of his life. Even with the thousands of unanswered questions and thoughts, I was glad to see everyone at Mom's celebration. I knew that some of the attendees were in the League. They moved and interacted like my Mom. They used their words carefully, knowing each had its own meaning.

I continue to scan the backyard until I felt this warm hand in mine. I look over to see it was Shad and he whispers to me, "Relax Lice. I can tell that you're tense a mile away and if I can tell, I know anyone else can tell. Celebrate Ma Angela today and worry about everything else tomorrow." I hated when he was right. I grip his hand and walk with him into my Mom's garden. It was the only place that brought me peace in her absence. Since she's been gone, I picked up her green thumb and maintained her garden. I even started one of my own.

"Thank you, Shad," I smile up at him.
"You know I got your back Lice," he said as he smiles back. I love this man, probably from the first time I laid eyes on him, well maybe the second. Actually, from the first time I saw him, I wanted to jump his bones. Then the second time I saw him, I wanted to marry him. But that's neither here nor there.

"How have you been? I haven't seen you lately."

"Well, you know Brian has us on tight shifts around here, people still want their wine, so I've been traveling a lot more. How about you? How have you been?"

"Haha, yea I know Pops does not play when it comes to his wine, his business, or his daughters so I understand. I've been good actually, I just finished the designs for a new hotel that they're going to be building uptown."

"Oh my god, that's so amazing! Congratulations Shad!"

"Congratulations indeed Rashad," said Grandma J as she walks into the garden.

"Well, Hello Grandma Jean, and thank you!"

"I'll always be proud of my grandson-in-law," smiles Grandma J. She loves her some Rashad. This little woman cussed me out so bad when I filed for a divorce, like my god, whose grandmother are you? Mine or his?

Grandma J. is an O.G. and my Mom's Mom. She practices hoodoo and voodoo. If you piss her off, she'll definitely give you a taste of the voodoo. Grandma J is from Barbados. I call her my Bajan queen. She and my grandfather, Poppy, a.k.a. Ronnie, migrated to America before my Mom, aunts, and uncles were born.

Poppy decided the states wasn't for him anymore, so he decided to return home to Barbados once all his kids were grown. Grandma J occasionally returns there to visit him and her other family members. Poppy only comes when he is forced by Grandma J or there is a threat to the family.

Angela Rosalyn Waytes is Grandma J's oldest daughter, and that Bajan blood runs deep. Mom used to tell me how she picked up so many traits from Grandma J. So, when I look at this little firecracker, barely standing 5 '0 feet tall, I know she knows more about Mom's life than anyone. I know she can answer some of my questions about what Mom was trying to do.

"You're doing it again Lice."

"Huh? Doing what?"

"You're in your head. Remember what I told you? Enjoy today. I'll catch you ladies later. I have an early day tomorrow."

There he was saving me from myself again. That's why I fell so hard for him and would give anything to protect him. Before I could finish watching him walk away, Grandma J grabs my hand and said, "Come with me, your mother would want you to have this."

"What is it?"

"Let's just say it's her little black book from The League. I have a feeling your mother was in too deep. She always told me to hold on to this book and flash drive in the event something happened to her and to give it to you when you were ready. You all were dealing with Angela's loss, so I held onto them until now."

"Grandma J, you should've told me about this! I could have been looking for her killer way before now." "Solice, there is a method to my madness. You should know that about your Grandma by now. My baby always found her way back to her family and I thought for sure this time she would come back by now, so I held on to her things."

"I understand."

Grandma J trusted my Mom's instincts so much. She was right, Mom always came home to us, regardless of whether she was beaten, bruised, or near death, she always came back. I took the book and flash drive home that night and went back through all her connections. I knew only Shunny could properly decode everything that was on the flash drive, so I would put her to work later.

I took some time to debrief my feelings for today. As I flip through her book, reading her notes, I began to feel the same rage I felt the day she went missing. Nothing added up. I had gone to her disappearance site a thousand times looking for clues and taking pictures. It was like the site was swept clean before we got there.

I think it was time that I revisited some of the evidence that the FBI had in my Mom's incident file. I needed to look over the investigators and who they are associated with. If they're connected to Nelson or the League someone better start answering some questions.

I put aside her book and begin making my connection board. I text Shunny and Uncle Jack to come over in the morning. My mind was in overdrive, so I decide to take Mina for a run. The moon was beaming bright and beautiful. It made me smile because it was always me and Shad's thing to stare at the moon. Hell, even my middle name was Luna, so it only made sense. With everything that was going on, I decide to send Shad the "you up?" text.

Rashad: Yea I'm Up... What's good?
Me: Look at the moon
Rashad: She's beautiful. Just like you. Why are you up?
Me: Out running with Mina and thinking about Mom
Rashad: Be safe Lice. I know things about Ma Angie still bother you and I also know that mind of yours is working in overdrive. Get some rest. Love u let me know when you're back in
Me: Love you too. Have a safe flight tomorrow

I finally make it back into the house and plop down on the bed. Tomorrow will be a long day. I wake up the next morning with my Uncle and my sister playing in my doorbell camera. They have a damn key and the code. These two are a special case just like Mom and Uncle Jack was. Thanks, Ma for always showing up when I need you. I grab my phone and unlock the door for them.

"I'm upstairs!"

"You didn't cook nothing? Dang sis and your fridge is always empty!"

"Haha, I can't stand you, lil girl. I'm never here!"

"But you sure aren't missing any meals because uhhhh, I think your butt is getting big."

"I'm about to put you out. Now come on so y'all can look at all these connections to Mom and Nelson. Sis, I need you to look at the stuff on this flash drive and try to hack into the FBI's file on Mom and research the investigators and look through their investigation reports. Both past and present to see if they have a pattern of covering information up. Uncle Jack, do you still know that guy that can recreate virtual scenarios?"

"Yea I will give him a ring and send him over the file once Shunny gets a hold of it."

"I'll work on reviewing the info on the flash drive and getting the file and info on the investigators A.S.A.P. I may have to get my home girl, Em, to help. They've been on high alert lately."

"Sounds good and while you do that, I'm going to hit up Aunt Max again to see what she remembers."

I call Aunty Max but no answer. She hadn't kept in contact with us as much since Mom's disappearance. Not sure if it was because of grief, remorse, involvement, or fear of being next if she got too close to us. Maybe I'll pop up on her one day to get some answers. Until then we'll keep working.

BRIAN WAYTES

It has been a long 7 long years without my baby. I miss her so much, but it brings me so much joy to see my girls. Solice looks just like her mother, except taller and goofier. Haha, I guess she gets that from me. I still remember the day I met Angela, she was in her Marine uniform, and good lord!... She was one of the baddest mama jammas I had ever seen in my 22 years of life. She was beautiful, and she had a gap when she smiled.

I had to travel to Germany for a boxing match and there she was in the bar where me and my trainer decided to go.

"Excuse me miss, can I..."

"No, you cannot, I don't accept drinks from strangers. Thank you.", she replied in the fieriest way.

"Well, Miss..." looking at her nameplate, "Sutton, I was only going to ask for you to pass me that menu behind you."

She was instantly embarrassed. I smiled to myself as she apologized and proceeded to hand me the menu.

"My name is Brian, and it's a pleasure to meet you, Miss Sutton. Thank you for all your hard work and be safe out there." She nodded with a smile, and I walked away.

I never thought I would see her again after that night. Little did I know, my Marine angel loved boxing and would be at my fight later that day. There I sat in my corner of the ring, and my trainer told me to look past him. I was confused at first, but when I looked past his shoulders, there she was.

Her hair was gelled down with a side part, she had on red lipstick, and a formfitting dress that showed off her beautiful shape. She saw me staring and quickly glanced away as if she was blushing. I knew I could not lose to this German punk. I had to show off my skills to Miss Sutton.

Once the fight began, me and old buddy danced around the ring a bit for the first couple of rounds, but it was time to get down to business. I had to show Miss Sutton why she should be on my arm, at least for our time in Germany. By the 3rd round, I knocked him out clean and looked over at Miss Sutton screaming in excitement. She ran up to the ring and slid me her number and she kissed me on the lips. Needless to say, she surprised the hell out of me.

She waited for me to change and come out of the locker room. We walked and talked for hours. We talked about our families, boxing, love, traveling, favorite foods, and future plans. She stayed over in the morning for a nap, and I watched her sleep for a little while. I knew my time in Germany was coming to an end soon. We agreed to do whatever it takes to be together.

I had never been so intrigued by a woman in my life. She loved life and her job so much. We dated on an international level. I was from Washington, D.C., so I would fly out of Dulles to meet her wherever she was, if she wasn't on a Special Ops mission. When she came home to Maryland, I would drive to her parents' house and vice versa. I scheduled my fights in places I knew she would be. She would take leave just to see me in D.C. or pop up at my dojo sometimes just to say "Hi B."

After about 2 years, I decided that it was time for me to pop the question. I planned everything as carefully as possible. I knew she was going to be headed to Barbados to spend time with her parents, so I lied and told her I couldn't make it because I had to travel for a match. Truth is, I was already in Barbados waiting for her.

I spoke to her father, Mr. Ronnie, and had him set up a fake boxing match and tell her he was going to take her. Then I asked Mama J to take her shopping and pick her out something pretty to wear. Later that night, both families were present at the ringside, but she didn't notice my family because she hadn't met them yet. She had only spoken with them on the phone.

The paid announcer called her to the ring to hold the "Round" cards and as she turned around, there I was, on one knee. "Angela my Angel, will you marry me?" She looked at me and screamed, "Hell yea I will! You liar!"

We got married the next day and headed back to D.C. the following week. That was one of the greatest moments of my life. Since the day I met her, I was living to see that smile of hers.

From that time on, I was fully aware of what I was getting myself into. We had an open-door policy in our marriage. I always asked Angela to tell me when our family was in danger. She never went back on that agreement. We trained together and we fought together. Sometimes I felt like I was married to two different people because she had a switch from our everyday life to killer instinct. I remember the first time we went on a "trip" to Lagos, Nigeria and it ended up being a mission.

We were walking out of our hotel room, and I heard a strange white man yell "Elle est lá! Tue-La! Tue-La!" Now I wasn't the best in French but being a boxer, many countries wanted their boxer to kill me from their embarrassment, so I understood what he said. We both began to run down the hallway.

"Angel, why in the hell are they yelling to kill you?!"

"Baby it's a long story!"

"Yea and you'll have to tell me about it, and soon!"

We headed to the staircase, and she stopped and pulled out a pistol with a silencer on it and shot two of the men trailing us. There were three more running up the steps towards us and I cold-cocked the first one and kicked the second one in the chest to knock him and the third one down the steps. Baby must've been in her groove once she saw I was on board. *Pop. Pop. Pop.* She shot all three of them. We kept on running. Once we found the laundry closet, we hid to regroup.

"Angela, what in the fuck was that? Baby, I told you to warn me when shit was going south."

"They made me, and I didn't know. I think it was a setup. I need to call Jack but first, we need to get our shit out of that room."

"I'll go get it."

"Hell no! I'm not letting you go back up there alone." She jumps up.

"Angela, I'm a grown man and I can handle myself, ya' dig? They are looking for you so why in the hell would I let you go back up there? I am your husband and I'm going to protect you with my life. Do you understand me?"

"Yes, I do." She looks shocked.

"Now call the police using the emergency phone near the elevator, in the lobby, and tell them you heard gunshots at the hotel so that some of the heat will die down. Then you come back to this closet and wait for me."

I had to laugh. She didn't even put up a fight because she trusted me. I found a janitor's uniform in the closet and slid out with the janitor's cart. I took the elevator back up to our floor. As I stepped off the elevator, my heart was pounding because I was praying no one had seen those bodies yet.

Luckily, they were still laying there, and I was able to get in the room and grab our stuff. I threw everything on the cart and headed back to the elevator. When I got back to the lobby, police were rushing into the elevator and shoving me out. That was perfect.

I hurried back to the laundry closet and closed the door.

"Angela"

"Brian?"

"Yes, baby it's me, here change your clothes and put this hat on."

"Did you grab my cell phone?"

"Here, take this big old thing." I toss it to her.

I'm not sure what type of access The League had but this cell phone predated its time. She called her brother, Jack, to help with our extraction plan and we were out of Lagos within 2 hours. Jack had arranged for us to go to Cape Town with a friend he served with. That had been one of the craziest times of my life.

My girls really think I don't know what their mother was into or what she was capable of. Hell, they even think I don't know what they do when they go on so-called business trips around the world. But the same way I let Angela live her life, is the same way I allow my girls to live their lives. I know they are surrounded by people who would stand up to the Devil himself for those girls. As their father, I am at peace with knowing that me and their mother trained them for every outcome. With that, I have no regrets.

SOLICE WAYTES

As a kid, I always wondered why in the hell did my parents want us involved in so much stuff. I just wanted to be a normal kid but here I was in French, Spanish, and German languages classes, along with swimming and learning martial arts. Where is the fun in any of that? Now I know, none of that was supposed to be fun, it was for training.

My parents had a plan for us, even before we were conceived, they knew what type of life they would have to prepare us for. Although we were pretty much free to make many of our own choices, being able to defend or protect ourselves and others was non-negotiable.

It was always family over everything and preserving the community over anything, by any means necessary. Pops' parents were lawyers, they did a lot of groundwork to stop gentrification in the DMV area. They loved our community so much. Grams and Papa used to tell us so many stories about Martin Luther King Jr., John Lewis, Huey P. Newton, Malcolm X, Muhammad Ali, and

Black Wall Street and how it was destroyed along with other prominent Black communities.

In those hard times, Papa turned to boxing. Papa was a self-taught boxer and he taught Pops when he wasn't in the courtroom. That's probably why he loved it so much. Grams became a Master Sommelier after she retired from practicing law. Papa saw how much joy it brought her, so they moved out of D.C. to Virginia to buy a farm and start Waytes Wines Enterprise. I come from a long line of established Black Royalty.

My grands and parents worked so hard to put the next generation ahead so we could escape the devil's grip of White Amerikkka. They never wanted their children or grandchildren to work for anyone other than their own people. It wasn't just about us though, both set of grandparents and our parents made sure they hired people who looked like us. This is how we live, this is how we survive.

Now that I look back, we were our own little Black Wall Street. My Uncle Jackson, my Mom's younger brother, owns a guns and tactical shop. Mom's sisters, Aunt Janice and Aunt Jeanette own a chain of hotels in the Caribbean Islands. Uncle Avery, Mom's oldest brother, is a technology specialist.

My Aunt Marie, Pop's sister, owns a small grocery store, and Uncle Tomas, Pops' younger brother is a lawyer. Grandma J still owns a metaphysical, herb, and health store. Like I said Grandma J is an O.G. Her connections with the ancestors and others who have passed on is majestic.

She always gives them the utmost respect through her prayers and libations. Every day she makes sure she prepares a meal for them to receive at the altar in her backyard. Grandma J even made sure she left one of her guns near the altar so they would feel safe in her presence. That ain't the only place Grandma J keeps a gat. She has one in damn near every room. I mean what can you expect from the first woman of our generations of assassins?

Back when Grandma J was around 16, her mother, my great-grandmother, Nanny, was kidnapped as leverage against The League because the United Kingdom caught wind of their involvement in trying to gain Barbados' independence from the UK's control. Grandma J's father, my great-grandfather, happened to be a founder and lead assassin in The League. My great-grandfather left Grandma J in charge of the other children while he went to go save their mother.

Unfortunately, she had to learn how to shoot, steal, and kill during the 6 months it took her father to extract her mother from the United Kingdom government. She also worked for a local Obeah practitioner which allowed her to learn herbalism, spells, and traditional Afro-Caribbean religious practices. This is how she learned to create her own medicines and poisons.

Once her father returned with their mother, he knew that their missions would only get more dangerous, so he began to train Grandma J the same way she trained my Mom and the same way my Mom trained me. Hell, Grandma J is the first person who put a gun in my hand. I was probably about 10 at the time when she said,

"Here, take this and shoot it."

"Shoot it?! Grandma J I don't know how to shoot a gun! I'm only 10." This woman handed me a sawed-off shotgun and told me to shoot it. Was she crazy?

"Soli shoot the damn gun girl!" I remember thinking, HERE GOES NOTHING! BOOM! I fell back with the first shot. It felt like I had dislocated my shoulder.

"GRANDMA J! WHY WOULD YOU MAKE ME DO THIS?!" She fell out laughing.

"Soli, please, you are overreacting. Didn't it feel good though?"

She has a point. It was the most freeing thing I had ever done and before I knew it, I learned to shoot everything in Uncle Jack's gun shop.

"Mama, the girls need to get ready for their Muay Thai lesson. That's enough guns for the day."

"Oh Angela, there's not enough time in the day for the number of weapons we have in here. Plus, next week's lesson is on poisonous plants. They should really enjoy that."

"Ma! You know there is more to preparedness than guns and poison."

"I train them to think too. Who do you think taught you?"

"Daddy, hahaha"

"Very funny, very funny. Go on girls, Grandma J will see you later."

"Bye Grandma J!"

Shunny and I ran out behind Mom. We dread Muay Thai. We were always so drained afterward.

"Mommyyyy, do we have to go?"

"Yes, Shunny, you have to go. Or do you want to tell your father that you don't think one of his crafts is important?"

"No Ma'am." She pouted and sat back in her seat.

"Alright, Let's roll!"

We were training to be and beat the best so I couldn't be mad at my parents for that.

I advanced quickly in Muay Thai and Mom figured it was time to start talking to me about the history of The League. For a child, it was mad overwhelming, confusing, and even kind of traumatic. I was told never to take on a task without knowledge of what you are walking into and if you do not know what you are walking into, you better plan like you do. Next, my training would focus on my psyche. Critical thinking was drilled into me and Shunny. So often that we would complain to our parents that our brains hurt.

"Girls, come here."

"Yes, Mom!" We both run into the study to see what Mom wants.

"Tell me, what are the key qualities of a critical thinker?"

"Oh, I know! A great researcher." Shunny said happily.

"Someone with foresight and can evaluate what they already have." I said proudly.

"You consider the consequences of each action you take."

"Active listening!" Soli shouted.

"Very good, my babies. I'm so proud of you. Here's a treat for you both", she smiled as she handed us hot chocolate and walked us to our bedroom. She leaned down to kiss each of us on our foreheads, then whispered in my ear that I would be hanging out with her, Grandma J, and Uncle Jack tomorrow. This would be the beginning of many "hangouts."

MADE WOMAN

It was time that we catapulted Soli into her real training. Jack and I were assigned to a job in Aruba to dead Romarie Morello. Normally I would go alone or with Jack, but Soli has been tagging along with us and learning defensive tactics since she was about 7 years old. She was more than prepared to handle her own in the field whether she thought it or not.

Either way, I was going to be right there to see my baby girl through this. First, I had to make sure we got there on time. She will complain that she has a class in the morning, but she will be fine. Let me call her and get her up.

"Hello?"

"It's time Soli, get up!"

"Maaaa?! It's 1am"

"Could you not be so loud? Get up and meet me at the gate outside of your dorm."

Click.

I wait as she strolls down to the gate with no sense of urgency. My child. I know she means well but she worries me sometimes. I even worry myself about the life I birthed her into. Sigh. She hops in and we head to the abandoned landing strip. Jack is there waiting on us in the helicopter and we set out to Aruba. I could tell her anxiety was settling in, but I knew she would breathe through it as she had learned in training. Meanwhile, I'm going to take a quick nap and maybe we'll be there by the time I awake.

I look over at my mom napping as we land in Aruba. I shake my head because here I was again with my crazy mother and her crazy brother. We head over to our rendezvous site and this time the cuckoo crew had me at a stakeout at 3 am near Romarie Morello's condo. Romarie covered up a lot of politicians' dirt whether it was murders, drugs, guns, black landowner theft, or big money schemes. You name it and she's probably covered it up. So many scandals never saw the light of day because of her. Unfortunately, she was too good at her job and even the best security wasn't going to stop this hit.

Mom and Uncle Jack have contacts in all the islands and the locals were loyal to them because they were like family. They gave us the best hideouts in exchange for resources for their communities. It was cool that they dragged me along, but sleep would've been much better considering it's a school night. I couldn't hang out on school nights in high school, but I guess it's all good now that I'm in college.

One thing about my mom and uncle, they believe in on the-job training, no matter the time, the place, or the person. Mind you, I am the type of college student that picks an 8 am class after being warned several times by my friends that it was a bad idea. And please believe my mother will have me back in the States on time for class because she does not believe in wasting education, for The League or anyone in that case. So here I am in an abandoned tower, with shades on acting like I am paying attention when really, I am dozing off.

"Aye sis, your pickney over there sleeping her training away."

"Soli!"

"YES! I'm up Ma." I look at her over my glasses.

"Child, why do you have sunglasses on in pitch dark? Looking like Stevie Wonder"

"I thought they were night goggles", she knew I was lying but let me have it.

"Uh huh, get over here and look at your target."

"M-M-My target?" I point at myself.

"Yes, Solice. You're our sniper today. Round of applause!" She claps dryly.

"Ma, I can't be a sniper! I'm good at close range shooting and poison."

"You're great at everything, Solice and just good isn't going to work in this profession. Now. Now, cut the small talk, and let's do this. Uncle Jack will coach you through it." I look over at Uncle Jack and look back at my mama.

"Guess there isn't any other option, huh?"

"Nope!", they both say as they laugh.

I walk over to the window where the sniper rifle is and get into position. It's windy outside but I figure it would be fine. The heat seeker is showing the target lying in bed and based on the heart rate she is completely asleep. As soon as I aim at Romarie, Uncle Jack stops me.

"Do you know why I just stopped you?"

"No, I thought all I had to do was shoot."

"Wrong. Do you see how hard the wind is blowing and all the trees swaying around that area of the house?"

"Yes, what about it?" I was confused.

"All of those factors can throw off your shot and cause you to miss. You want to wait until it is still. Or if it's in the middle of a storm or just windy you need to make sure you account for that before making a shot. All elements need to be included in your equation."

"Unc now you know, I'm no good at math."

"You better learn this type of math, your life will depend on it. Seconds. Minutes. Hours. Wind Speed. Breaths. Body positioning. Everything in your environment matters. The sooner you learn that the better sniper you will be. Most importantly, have patience. Now try again."

I take a deep breath and check my surroundings. I make sure my stand has proper positioning and my scope is zeroed in on Romarie. I take another deep breath and look through my scope while waiting for the perfect moment. Sweat starts to roll down the back of my neck and my back. My anxiety is at an all-time high because if

I mess this up, we could be caught. The wind continues whipping back and forth. My breaths become shakier, and the top of my lip began to sweat. I start doing my breathing exercises. Inhale 1, 2, 3, 4. Hold.

Exhale 1, 2, 3, 4, 5... Suddenly, the winds stop. Romarie turns to her side. Deep breath, one eye closed the other eye in the scope. I pull the trigger. *Swoosh*. The bullet hit her in the back of the head.

"Pack it up let's go!", Mom shouts but I was still stuck. Uncle Jack was breaking down the stand and then taking the rifle from my grip.

"Solice! Let's go! Now!" I snap out of it and run behind them. My heart was racing, and my world was spinning as we continue to run down the stairwell.
Once at the bottom of the stairs, a van was waiting on us.

We hop in and the road to a hidden helipad. We get into the helicopter and just like that we're out. Heading back to Maryland. It was a silent ride home for me. Mom and Unc knew it was a first for me and it was nothing they could say to ease what I just experienced. I finally fell asleep on the way back.

When I woke up, it was 7:30 am and we are landing at a private airstrip at one of Uncle Jack's friends. "Come on Soli. You have 30 minutes before class starts. Go shower and I brought you some clothes from home." I nod and go to shower in Uncle Jack's friend's house. I scrubbed my whole body so hard that I thought that I would start bleeding.

Although I didn't get a speck of blood on me, I felt dirty and bad. I get out of the shower and look at myself in the mirror. I didn't know who I was looking at. I comb my hair and brush my teeth then ran to my mom's car. She looks over at me as we began to drive and reaches over to grab my hand. I squeeze her hand.

"I love you, babygirl."

"Love you too, Mom."

"I push you because I want you to survive. This life is not easy. Doing this job makes it much harder. I want to prepare you in every way possible. We do what we do to bring peace to the people who look like us. People hate us for no reason and try everything they can to hurt us, but we always rise. I hope that you will escape this life and be happy. Be in love. Even when the rest of the world doesn't love us, I want you to seek love in yourself. This morning was hard for you, and I know that. But baby this is just a job. That woman has covered up so much hatred and lack of accountability and profited from it."

"I know it has to be done Ma. I just don't want to lose myself in this."

"Then don't. Prioritize your mental health while you do this job. Meditate and rest. And always remember that it is just a job like anything other job". She knew damn well our job was not like anyone else's. But she was right, I had a job to do. We pull up to campus and she kisses me on the forehead before I got out. I run to my Humanities class.

"You are late Ms. Waytes, please be seated."

"It's 8 am on the dot Professor Alexander."

"To be on time is to be late."

"But that makes no sense, to be on time is to be on time."

"If you want to be prepared and check out your surroundings and competition you should always be early rather than on time. Now be seated without disturbing others."

I roll my eyes and go to sit in the back. After the morning I had, Professor Alexander could save all his B.S. philosophy. I hadn't heard a word he said from that point on.

"Ms. Waytes, you seem to be in deep thought so tell me, what is your resolve?"

"My what?"

"What is your RESOLVE Ms. Waytes? Your determination. Your drive. What fuels you to keep going?"

"Is that a trick question?" I look around the classroom and then back at Mr. Alexander. He stares at me. I sit up in my chair to speak.

"Umm, well. I guess my resolve would be to find some way to bring peace to the world of people who look like us. We never really have a chance to find that because every other month one of us has been killed or murdered with no accountability held for the murderer. We live in a constant state of trauma, with no room to heal. We're mocked for what we look like but if a white woman or man copies our style it's all good.
Drugs and guns are dropped into our communities, but they continue to call us drug addicts and violent but not looking at how those things make it into our community. They normalize us killing each other in our own music

and we jam to it. We'd rather fight each other than fight the oppressor. I guess what I'm trying to say is, my resolve is to restore the pride and love we once had for one another. The compassion we had to protect each other. If that makes sense."

"Very good Ms. Waytes. I'll expect you to tell me more about that in you all's final assignments that are due next week."

It was the end of the semester and here Professor Alexander is trying to teach us about having a resolve. My resolve would carry me throughout my missions and life. Outside of school, work, and The League, I don't have a life. I guess I need to start having more of a social life with summer on the horizon. It's going to be summer, Solice. I'll make plans with the cousins and my girls next weekend after the wine festival. Duty calls for Waytes Wines. Maybe I'll see something cute out there.

SOLICE MEETS A KING

"Hey Pops, Can we set up on the side where the Ferris wheel is?"

"Sure, go ahead and find a spot. Me and Mom will finish bringing the products over. Here take the tent and the sign."

I grab the stuff from Pops and head over to our set-up location. As I look around, everything and everyone was so beautiful. It kinda reminds me of Summer of Soul but for wine instead of music. There were local performers and food trucks everywhere. Mom and Pop came over to help me finish setting up and then they vanished.

I turn around and there he was looking like a dark chocolate Godiva God in the summertime. He had a baby face. This was before everyone started rocking beards. He had the most beautiful jet-black wavy hair I'd ever seen. Thick lips that would be perfect on mine. The sexiest smile that could melt your panties right off. He has to be standing at about 6 '5. Damn who is he? *Mmmm Mmmm Mmmm*. He could easily be Kofi Siriboe's finer brother.

I'm stuck at the table being a wine vendor for my parents while they mingle with restaurateurs and other patrons. I've seen his parents before at other wine festivals, but they never stopped by our table. I can tell they loved the wine festival as much as they loved supporting black-owned businesses, so they had to stop my way this time.

"Hello, I'm Solice, and welcome to the Waytes' Wines Experience. We currently have our Signature Rose', Merlot, Moscato, and Pinot Grigio blends available for tasting. Which Signature Blend would you all like to try?"

"Ooohhhh Rashad, she is so adorable and polite. She would be perfect for you." *Hmmm. So, his name is Rashad.*

From this moment, I knew Mrs. Rebecca was going to be a problem. I look at her in shock and before I could say anything… "Ummm Ma can you try not to be so embarrassing? She looks like the type of young woman who would say what she wants."
No, this negro just didn't put me on the spot. Just who in the hell did he think he was?

"You're absolutely right sir, and I'm sorry ma'am but I like women and you're kind of cute too." I say jokingly to Mrs. Rebecca.

"Well, Rebecca, I bet you didn't see that coming, Did ya?" He and his dad laugh as Mrs. Rebecca turns red as an apple.

"Hi young lady, I will take a Pinot and Mrs. Rebecca will take a Rose' since it seems as though the cat has her tongue, and she can't order. We're the Kings, by the way, I'm Clint and this is our son Rashad."

"It's a pleasure to meet you all, here are your samples and please don't be a stranger." I smile as I hand them their cups and I catch Shad staring at me. Looks like he was interested after all because he decided to come back by my booth.

"You like women, huh?"

"Haha, what's it to you, uhhhh Richard?", I knew damn well what his name was, fine as he is, I would never forget his name.

"RICHARD?!, Haha, you got more jokes huh," he licks his lips then sizes me up like he wants to have me for dinner. I instantly got wet, and that shit hadn't happened in a while. This man didn't even have to touch me and there I was dripping.

"You know *damn* well you heard my loud ass Mama say "Oooooh Rashad." I giggle a little.

"Sir, I have served a lot of people today, what possibly made you think that I would remember your name?"

"Oh, so we're playing hard to get huh, Solice? See, I remembered your name?"

"Well, Rashad, that's easy because I have a name tag on," I stated as I pointed to my name tag.

"True True, but I definitely didn't remember your name because of that. I can't even lie, you're fine as hell."

"Well thank you, this look is courtesy of Angela and Brian Waytes, thank you very much."

"No disrespect, I just think you're beautiful. I tell you what, take my number and if you decided to call later, I'll pick up." He grabs my phone and calls his number from it. I had to smirk because it was the cutest, most cliche move ever. As he walks away, the scent of his cologne faded slowly.

My parents finally decided to make their way back to our booth.

"I just want yall to know, I need some overtime pay! It is hot out here and all the winos are out here living their best lives and getting on my nerves."

"Soli you are *soooo* dramatic," Mom laughs as she helps me pack up the bottles.

"Go ahead and get out of here Soli, me and Mom will take care of the rest."

I hug my parents and decide I will hang out at the Harbor for a while tonight. As I was walking back to my car and texting my cousins, I bumped into Shad.

"Damn could you watch...." He turns around and looks at me.

"You must be stalking me today, Rashad."

"Solice" he smirks.

"Where are you headed?"

"I'm meeting my cousins at pizza joint around the way, let me guess you wanna come?"

"Nah, I want you to hang with me."

"Now how do I know you're not a killer?"

"How do I know you're not one?" Well damn, he read me well. Nobody knew except my Mom, Uncle, and Grandma J.

"I'm not. So, I guess I can hang out with you. No funny business though."

"I'll be a perfect gentleman. My dorm isn't too far from here."

"I have my own dorm, Rashad."

"Oh word, where do you go to school?"

"I go to Bowie State, how about you?"

"I'm a junior at Bowie State, but I recently transferred here from Norfolk State University."

"Oh lord, you're a retired Spartan. This is going to be a long night." I go with him back to his dorm. It was actually pretty clean, plus he was a resident assistant, so he had his room all to himself. I can't lie, I was already hot for him by the time we got to his room. So of course, in true Summer, Solice fashion, I had to make the first move.

I grab his hand and lean in for a soft kiss. As I close my eyes, I thought to myself, *Got damn! His lips are so soft!* We stare into each other's eyes for a second and he goes in for the next kiss. By the time he pulls his tongue out of my mouth, I was on fire. I couldn't even control my own vagina. She starts jumping and juicing at the same time. He picks me up and wraps my legs around his waist then carries me to his bed.

"Are you sure you want to do this, Solice?"

"I know what I'm doing, Rashad." I kiss him again as he lays me down on the bed. He then began to kiss my neck as he ran his soft hands up my dress and pulls my panties off. I couldn't wait for him to put his hands and lips all over me. He slowly continues to undress and kiss me. Once he finishes taking my dress off, he licks and sucks my rock-hard nipples.

"I've been waiting to put my mouth on these since I first saw you."

I tremble as he blew on my nipples while gently rubbing my clit. I know he feels me gushing uncontrollably. I think that shit turned him on more than it did me. I just have to see his naked body, so I pull his shirt off and push his basketball shorts down. I bite my lip as I look at his beautiful body as the moonlight glistened on his dark chocolate skin through his dorm window. I ran my fingertips down from his chest to his 6-pack and down to the elastic band in his boxers.

The suspense of what he was hiding in his boxers was killing me. I reach into his boxers and pull out a third leg. He was watching me so I knew I couldn't punk out. Before I could rub it against my clit and between my throbbing lips, he stops me and pushes my legs back beside my head. From the way he kissed me earlier, I already knew he was about to lick my soul out of my body.

Those soft lips met my clit with a French kiss. He sucked and licked my clit like it was a Tootsie Pop and he wanted to see how many licks it would take for me to cum. By the time I start shivering into my first orgasm, he switches it up and slid his rock-hard dick inside of me. I lost it! I start trembling and crying like a damn fool as he strokes me slowly.

"Am I hurting you?! I can stop."

"NO...DON'T...STOP!" I could barely breathe. He literally took my breath away. Once he saw I was fine, he flips my ass over and slides back inside of me. I arch my back so I could take all of him. He's acting like he is having the time of his life smacking my ass and listening to me moan. He finally came, but his dick was still hard, and I want more. As he fell backward, I climb on top of him and slide down on that pole.

It's my turn to be in control. He fondles and licks on my breast as I slide to the tip of his dick and slam back down. Now he is the one moaning. Every time I slide down, I tighten my warm, gushy walls around his shaft. That shit is driving him crazy. I know he is ready to cum again once he held me tight, then we came together. After the first time, we became in sync when we made love. He is never too rough or too gentle. There is a fire chemistry between us.

We shower and he orders us some Philly cheese steaks and fries. We sit and talk about our dreams and goals. He is pretty smart and studying to be an architect. We watch my new favorite movie, Love Jones. What really got me was the posters he had on his walls. There is one by Fred Hampton that said, 'I was born in a bourgeois community and had some better things in life, but I found that there were more people starving than there were people eating, more people that didn't have clothes than did have clothes, and I just happened to be one of the few. So, I decided that I wouldn't stop doing what I'm doing until all those people are free.'

"That's so beautiful." I am in awe of this statement because this is something my parents preached to me and my sister all the time. Until we're all free none of us are free.

"Yea man, my grandparents were a part of the Black Panther Party back in the day. My granddad and Mr. Hampton was cool." His people were just like mine. They taught him the same values and beliefs. It is rare to find people who actually get you.

"You're going to be my wife, Solice." I look at this man like he is crazy, and he knew he sounds crazy.

"How do you know that, Rashad?"

"Most men know and I'm telling you I know."

"I guess you'll just have to prove it to me."

"I plan on it. What are you doing for the rest of the weekend?"

"Well, I had plans to hang with my family tomorrow."

"Take me with you. I want to meet my future in-laws."

"You're future in-laws? Haha, laying it on thick, aren't you?"

"Not at all. Now, would you like to spend the night here and I take you to your dorm to get some clothes in the morning?"

I nod with a smile, and we lay down to go to sleep. When we wake up in the morning the sun is beaming through the window. I sit up and look at his beautiful face.

God, he is fine. Most guys my age are shallow, and very shallow if they are fine. I look out the window and sigh.

"What's wrong, Beautiful?"

"Oh, you're up. Good Morning!"

"Good morning, yea I'm up. You sigh loud as hell, haha."

"HAHA, you're not funny, Rashad. I did not sigh that loud!"

"You do get pretty loud when I... Well, you know."

"Funny guy this morning huh?"

I push him back down and he pulls me down with him then kisses me. It still felt like butterflies this morning so it couldn't be a one-off. I notice every time I kiss him, his third arm stands straight up.

"You don't have to stare baby girl. You can have it whenever you like. Matter fact let me do all the work this time."

And we are back at it again like rabbits. If we keep this up, we're definitely going to miss the cookout.

"Boy, we have to stop! Look at the time. You have held me hostage in this room all morning."

"You wanted round 2 and I aim to please. We can go though. Come on we can hit the shower and you can wear something of mine until we get back to your room."

"Keep your hands to yourself in the shower."

"I can keep my hands to myself, but I don't know about my lips, and you know you and him have become very acquainted between last night and this morning."

I smile as he leads me to the shower. He turns the water on and hops in. I watch the water run down his body and I really start to question if we're going to make it to my parents. He pulls me in the shower and begins to wash my body. It feels like heaven being pampered. I begin to wash him, committing every inch of his body to memory. *Woo!* How haven't I seen him on campus before?

After we shower, he grabs me a t-shirt and some basketball shorts. We walk out of his room, and he grabs my hand. I look up at him and he smiles, like he is totally comfortable and I am his girl. We walk to his car, and he opens my door then I hop in. When we arrive to my dorm, all my girls are sitting outside. Walk of shame here goes nothing. I step out of the car, and they automatically notice me. *Aww hell!*

"Tsk. Tsk. Tsk, Sis. Where have you been! I see that fine ass R.A. What's his name?" Rita scrunches up her face at me.

"Girl shut up," These heifers start waving and smiling at him while he's in the car.

"Will y'all come on. Soooo embarrassing!" I grab Rita by her arm and rush inside.

"Solice gotta a mannnnnn at homeeeee, or in the carrrrr!"

"I'm going to run away from y'all!"
I run through the front door, and they follow me to my room.

"Spill the tea, Sis," says Destiny as she lays across my bed.

"Right, because you are glowing and we have never seen you like this," Lena smiles at me as she nudges me.

"Okay! Okay! So, we just met yesterday...."

"YESTERDAY!!" They all shout together.

"Do y'all want the tea or not because I sense some judgment here."

"Judgment free zone. Please continue spilling."

"Thank you! I was working my parent's vendor table at the Harbor Wine Festival and he and his parents came over. He was throwing hella vibes my way, but you know I had to play hard to get a little bit. So, when I was leaving, he was leaving too, and we started chatting again and I found out he goes here."

"Uh-huh and that's why we didn't see you last night," Rita interjects.

"Girl, hush and let her finish," Lena sits on my bed and crosses her legs.

"He invited me to hang out with him and I figured why not. It's been a long semester. He's fine. My kitty is purring. I'm like cool, it'll be a one-night stand and I'll never see him again. No commitment, just a little fling. So, boom, we get to his room and it's clean and enlightening in there. We talk and he's actually smart. ALSO, a complete gentleman. At this point, I'm dripping wet. GIRLS! This man turns me out then tells me I'm going to be his wife."

"WIFE???" They yell again. Destiny is clutching her imaginary pearls.

"Yes, his wife. And he wants to meet the family today."

"Damn Solice. You didn't even leave in the middle of the night like you usually would! He must got that yemmy ya ya yay aye aye!" Lena says while body rolling.

"He's different. And y'all know, I don't bring anyone home."

"Yea, girl. We've been friends since elementary school and your family is crazy. He must really like you," Destiny is so hype. I have to laugh.

We keep talking while I get dressed. The girls and I walk out of the dorm and there he is sitting patiently. I hop in the car, and he flashes that gorgeous smile at me.

"Hey, Beautiful"

"Hey, Handsome!"

"Are you ready?" I nod and put the address in his GPS. He grabs my hand, then we're on our way. The closer we got to my parents' house the more my palms began sweating. I think he notices because he kisses my hand.

When we pull into the driveway, I take a deep breath while he gets out to open my door. He grabs my hand to help me out of the car then pulls me close to kiss my lips.

"Thanks for the invite"

"Sure thing, Hubby."

"Finally catching on huh, Wifey?" I smile.
We walk inside the house together.

"Hello! Where is everyone?"

"We're back here!" I hear Mom call out. We walk to the back yard and there everyone is, laughing, joking, playing games and happy. As soon as they look up and see us, they stop and stare.

"Well, look what the cat drug in. Come on out you two," Pops says as he is cooking on the grill.

"Pop, this is my friend…"

"Boyfriend," he says, and I look up at him. He flashes that smile.

"This my boyfriend, Rashad King." It was like that scene from Martin when he and Gina first met.

Pops looks at me with a surprised face and says, "Boyfriend, Rashad King. Nice to meet you, young fella. You must be something special if this one brought you home. Welcome to the family!"

"Hi, Rashad. I'm Mrs. Angela. Solice's mother. Thank you for coming," she smiles and hugs him. He was eating it up.

"Now tell me one thing son. Can you play spades?" *Oh lord, Pops. Why? Please say yes!*

"Oh, yes sir. It is a tradition in my family."

"Maybe you can help my daughter."

"Help me? I know how to play Pops!"

"Uh-Huh" He whisks Rashad away to the playing table.

"Pops! Really?"

Once he became Pops' spade partner, I knew I would never be able to get rid of him. That might not be a bad thing. They had so much fun with him. Even Grandma J, she loves him already. Over the next couple months, we always made time for one another. Whether it was at each other's parents' houses or cafeteria dates on campus, we love us. My missions, his internships, or summer break couldn't stop us. I feel safe with him.

Looking back at how we met, Shad and I were never supposed to fall in love. I intended to just have a one-night stand after meeting him at the National Harbor Wine Festival during summer break. He asked Mom and Pops if he could have my hand in marriage in October.

And as crazy as it sounds, right before Thanksgiving break, we ran off to elope in Niagara Falls. I married my best friend and King at the age of 20. Who would've thought? Surprisingly, none of our parents were surprised about what happened. It seems like they weren't the only ones with whirlwind love.

THE LEAGUE

I was always being trained for greatness. I was being trained to be a member of The League and to go beyond The League. As a black woman, I always was taught to go above and beyond my peers. I had to be the best to beat the best.

The League of Black Assassins. This included Black and Brown people from all walks of life from all over the world. Africa, the Americas, the Caribbean, London, Japan, you name it. There's only one way in and one way out. To become a member, you must be recommended by a current member, to end your membership, you must recommend another qualified person to take your spot.

There are no exceptions to The League's membership rules. Once sworn in, you take an oath of loyalty and secrecy. Rule #1: You are not to put any other organization's needs or duties above The League's. Rule #2: The world outside of The League does not know of its existence and in the event of a breach, the breaching party will be terminated.

Every morning I would have to tell Mom the goal of The League.

"Tell me Solice, what is the goal of The League we serve?"

"To build generational power for Black and Brown people around the world."

"Through what means?"

"Through skill and knowledge."

"Which does what?"

"Enables us to outsmart the enemy, neutralize threats, and protect and secure the future of others in our communities."

"What happens to those who come against us?"

"They shall perish by the strength of my hand and their souls will feel the raft of our ancestors."

"Very good baby girl. Now you can go back to sleep." She would smile and kiss me on my forehead.

As a member, you receive a couple of things: An off the grid phone that uses only mini phone towers that can bypass government receivers, an electronic blackout list with information about your hit, a secret bank account that is maintained in banks as "trust funds" a.k.a. money transferred from hit's accounts into The League's assets, transportation connections in each location, and a specially designed suit to protect against blades and bullets. But your training consists of arms handling, combat skills, and knowledge. Neither is greater than the other.

You also must decide on your specialty, as you will be trained in this field for several months before you are assigned your first mission. Since Grandma J was an herbalist, poison was an easy choice for me. I was already skilled in hand-to-hand combat due to my martial arts training and sparring with my parents. I am also a weapons specialist thanks to Uncle Jack. Poison was completely new to me.

Grandma J was too eager and happy for me to take on her specialty, of course. Mom wanted me to be a weapons specialist and proficient in hand-to-hand combat.

"Now Soli, I've always told you that if you can't get to any of your weapons you will have to fight your way through."

"Yes, Mom I know."

"Even though you work with Pops at the dojo, it is not enough to only scratch the surface. Training your body for the worst conditions and treatment is a constant thing. You my dear have to…"

"Train to beat the best."

"That's my girl! You and your sister make me so proud!"

I've had my ass kicked to get to this point. Everything from waterboarding to electrocution to poison, I have experienced it. Luckily Grandma J helped me build immunity for most of the commonly used poisons. She always taught me to look at my surroundings to find an herb or plant or something that can be of use to me. Being an assassin isn't easy, but someone has to do it.

Most of my missions began during my sophomore year at Bowie State. This was before Shad, and I met. They were easy missions at this point because I was under the scope of Mom. She basically ran D.C. for The League. My job was to plant listening devices for us to gain information on closed political meetings. From being a waiter to a maid, I had to always complete my missions, by any means necessary. By any means necessary sometimes meant being thrown out of places or putting yourself in danger.

I would always show up to my dorm room looking half dead but thankfully my roommate, now best friend, Lena, would always be out partying so she didn't see the worst of it. Whenever she would see me beat up, I would always lie and say it came from training at the dojo with Pops. She helped patch me up for the most part.

"Maybe you need to tell your Dad to take it easy on you. Wanna go get some lunch from the café?"

"He is very serious about his craft. He treats me just like his students. Sure, let's go."

"Girl, that's scary. I'm not sure I want to meet him."

"To know him is to love him."

"Solice, there goes your boo, Malcom" I honestly couldn't stand Malcom, but I was nice to him for my mission. He was a young Clarence Thomas. He was the president of the Young Republicans on campus and a political science major. He also had access to Keatley Wilson, a lead investigator for the Department of Justice, who was coming to speak at a panel later today. Although

Keatley worked for the Department of Justice he seldomly did anything to effectuate justice. He was the textbook liar and a cheat. He would cover up, hide, and overlook evidence, especially when it came to investigating violations of our rights or murders. He had senators, mayors, and judges in his pockets.

He was one of Mom's targets. I was a part of the panel set-up team for the Young Republicans. That meant I had to put a tracker on him by any means necessary. This was way before all the tech we have now, but hell it was a little more exciting. Uncle Jack provided me with different items that he was likely to pick up and take with him. I took all of them with me to the panel.

"Hey Solice. Make sure that you are on time this evening. Our guest is very important."

"Sure thing, Malcom. What else do you need?"

"Please be presentable. We must ensure we make him feel at home here at Bowie State. Show that HBCU pride!"

"I meant what else did you need for the panel?" I roll my eyes at him.

"Oh, you know. Water, pens, pads, and maybe a Bowie State welcome bag. You know make it work, you're a smart girl. Don't make us look bad." I nod because that was the only thing, I could do to stop myself from cussing his black ass out.

"Girllll, you better than me because I would have to whoop his ass."

"Believe me. It's for the greater good that I don't punch him in his shit. He's right. I'm a smart girl and my mom told me to explore all aspects of politics to know how they think."

"Your mom is so bomb. I just love her!" Haha, if only she knew that's who is kicking my ass most of the time. We sat in the café and chatted for a while. Then it was time for me to start getting ready for my mission, so I go back to the dorm and put on some slacks and a button-up. I slick my hair back in a bun and put my glasses on. Unc gave me a nice pen that was bugged and equipped with the tracker. Most people couldn't resist a nice pen so that would be my first option.

Next, I would be the one that hands him the clicker for his presentation. Grandma J made some type of concoction to spray on it to get his fingerprints. It looks like Lysol but was far from it, after an hour the spray would peel off, and allowed her to make gloves with his exact fingerprint. I put all types of trackers and bugs in the welcome bag. I knew I would also be the greeter so I would try to plant a tracker in the door handle of his car when I opened the door.

I head to the student union for the setup. I place his pen and pad in front of his seat and then go to the side door. The other tracker is activated by saliva, basically gum. I made sure I chewed it up and spit it in my hand while walking up to the SUV. His detail hopped out on my ass so fast.

"Stop right there young lady!" Oh, Shit they saw me. Ma is going to kill me.

"Yes, sir?"

"We will open Mr. Wilson's door."

"Oh sorry, no problem. He's our guest so I am being polite."

"Lead us inside."

Well, that failed. I turn around and lead them into the student union. This fool acted like he was the president in the way he waved at the crowd. Once at his seat, I saw how impressed he is with the pen. Looks like we have a winner. I sprayed the clicker and then walked over to hand it to him. The other panelist began to get seated, and I am praying that we didn't go over an hour because that would be my ass if they saw the film peel off the clicker.

After about 45 minutes of this boring ass panel, it is finally over. He takes the pen, and I lead them back to the SUV. I text mom an asterisk to let her know that he is on the move. She calls me.

"Solice I'm coming to get you. Uncle Jack is tracking Wilson."

"Whaaaa? Coming to get me? Where are you?"

"Meet me on Loop Road."

"Maaaa! What the heck?"

I start running to Loop Road and there she is on a motorcycle waiting on me.

"Where are we going?"

"SOLICE GET YOUR ASS ON AND LET'S GO!"

She throws me the helmet and I hop on. This lady pulls off so fast that I almost fall backward. My mother is obviously crazy. She's talking to my Uncle in her headset while going 120 mph. Before I know it my Uncle's pick-up truck is cutting off Wilson's SUV and the passenger window went down. He is firing shots at the SUV and I can't believe my eyes. Mom stops the bike and tells me to go hide in the bushes. Then she drives up beside the SUV to check for signs of life and Wilson happened to be the only one alive. That's when I learned my uncle is a master marksman.

Mom pulled Wilson out of the SUV with a .22 to his head then she threw a bag over his head. Uncle Jack threw him in the bed of the truck and covered it back up then got in the truck and left. These two were less subtle in their operations. She ran back to her bike and motioned for me to come on.

I hopped back on, and we followed Uncle Jack to their safe house. This had been the wildest day of my life so far and it wasn't because I was partying. My Friday night will consist of me helping Mom and Uncle Jack torture someone.

"Take his ass in there and tie him up."

"10-4 Sis."

"So, Mr. Wilson, is it? We haven't formally met, have we?" She makes sure I am out of his sight then she pulls the bag off his head. She takes her helmet off and smiles at him.

"What do you think you're doing? You'll never get away with this."

"Honey, they all say that. Now what you're going to do is give me all your assets, files, contacts, and contracts."

"I'm not giving you shit! You can burn in hell you BLACK BITCH!"

"Now now…Why couldn't I just be a regular bitch? I have to be a 'BLACK BITCH'"

"I'll call you nigg…"

Before I could blink, she has a blade to his throat.

"I just know a man in your position shouldn't use that word."

"I-I-I-I apologize", he took a big gulp.

"Humbling, isn't it? This Black Bitch is going to end your life as you've ended others' lives who look like me. But first, we need information". Uncle Jack comes up and sticks him in the neck with a truth serum. They took the fingerprint film from me and scanned a copy of his eyes and voice.

"Put the bag back on his head. Baby girl, you know what's better than a finger film?"

"Uh, the actual finger?" I look at her.

"Smart girl. Cut his middle finger and thumb off."

"Who? Me?" I point to myself.

"Who else, love?"

I look at her like she is crazy, and he starts screaming. This is the first time I looked at my mother like I didn't know who she is.

"Uhhh with what?"

"Take your pick." I walk over to the weapons wall and pick out a machete.

"Girl, are you cutting fingers or arms?"

"I mean you told me to pick" She gave me that look, and I go and pick up some wire cutters. I walk over to him and look at her. She motions for me to go ahead. I cut his thumb off and blood shoots everywhere. I gag. Now she's staring at me and he's screaming like he's dying. I close my eyes and cut the middle finger. I throw up on him. Uncle Jack bursts out laughing and I'm still throwing up. Mom is shaking her head.

"Y'all let's go. Let him sit here for a few days. I'll send Mommy over here to patch him up, so he won't die."

"Umm Mom, why did you need his middle finger too?"

"Oh hahaha, that was a final fuck you from this black bitch. You should drink something you lost a lot of fluids back there. We have another wine festival tomorrow in Virginia and you know your daddy doesn't play when it comes to Waytes Wines. You should get some rest tonight and a good dinner. Want me to cook?" She's crazy. She guided me out of the door.

"Uh whatever you cook is fine Mom."

We go home like nothing happened. Wilson being missing is all over the news, turns out they disabled all cameras in the area, so no footage of the disappearance was caught. Mom and Unc have one hell of a clean-up crew because they didn't even leave a trace of his detail or the SUV. This wouldn't be the last time the "Cuckoo Crew" would pull me into some insanity. Looking back, I wish I would've enjoyed those times with her more.

SHE'S POISON

My alarm blared with *Poison* playing. I hurried to turn it off before Shad woke up. It was 5 am and I had to start my day off getting prepared for what was ahead of me. I sat there and watched him sleep for a second before I started to meditate. My mind began to wander about my life. I bought the best suits, the nicest combat gear that Uncle Jack could supply, my favorite car, an Audi A7, the beautiful home on the outskirts of D.C., our red Doberman, Mina, and I had the finest husband in the world.

I had to scoff at my damn self. Sometimes doing for the greater good can destroy you. I loved my husband and I used to tell him everything, but how could I tell him that his wife was an assassin? I'm not even sure what that would do to him, knowing that he couldn't protect his wife. Or could he? Am I not giving the love of my life enough credit?

These are the same thoughts that raged last night. I was scheduled to go on my first high-level mission. I had to fly out to Italy for Pops and The League. That's the way it normally happens. I get an assignment in every place I have to travel to handle the wine business. This is done for me to keep a low profile. They have connections in TSA to ensure my equipment and weapons passed through without a problem. Luckily my hit, Sergio Cena, was on my flight and I just so happened to land a seat across the aisle from him on the plane.

He was your typical high-powered and entitled white man. A Mid-60s, white hair, tired-ass blue Tom Ford suit with a red tie and white button up. The same get-up I have been seeing all my life. I could feel him peering over at me and wondering why I was in first class along with him. He was extremely rude to the stewardess. He deserved everything that was coming to him, and I figured this would be an easy merk because Grandma J had put ricin in a tiny capsule for me to drop in his drink.

I had to be strategic and smart about how I did this to make sure it took effect in time. Typically, ricin could take up to 3 days to be effective but Grandma J tweaked it so it would kill in at least an hour, so I had to make sure I got it into his system before the end of the flight. Pops would kill me if I missed the International Wine Tourism Conference so I could not do it a moment too soon and risk the plane taking an emergency landing. Based on my case file, he loved to drink, so I had to make nice with the stewardess.

As I got up to go to the bathroom, I noticed them standing in a corner talking, so I decided to interject.

"Hi, I just want to say on behalf of the rest of the pleasant flyers in First Class, that we appreciate everything you ladies are doing, and that guy is a total dick."

"OH MY GOD, yes, he is a complete dick. Thank you so much for the compliment."

We exchanged smiles and I headed to the bathroom. I took out the ricin capsule to make sure it was secure, then ran the water to make it appear as if I had used the bathroom. As I walked out of the bathroom, the pilot announced that we were about 30 minutes away from landing, so I had to make my move.

"Excuse me miss, I know we only have a few minutes left before landing so to make it painless as possible, send the dickhead a drink on me and tell him that it's courtesy of the airline for their first-class flyers."

"Are you sure? I wouldn't give him anything."

"Absolutely, that should at least keep him off of your backs for the rest of the flight."

"Okay! One glass coming up."

She pulled out a bottle of Chardonnay and I knew I had to distract her to drop the ricin in, so it dissolved immediately. She poured his glass, and I slid the ricin to my fingertips.

"Could I have a glass as well?"

"Oh, sure! White or red?"

"Either is fine."

As she reached to grab me a bottle of Pinot, I quickly dropped the ricin in his glass.

"Here you go ma'am, thank you so much again."

"No worries." I smiled and walked away with my glass. She brought him his glass and he happily took the gesture. For the next 25 minutes, I was a complete wreck. Under my suit jacket, I was sweating bullets and wondering if I could pull this off. While the plane was beginning to land on the runway, and I was grabbing my carryon, I noticed he started to look a little pale.

"Will you hurry up! I need to get off this plane!" he began to shout.

I figured he was starting to feel the effects. As we were exiting the plane, he started to groan and lose his balance. Before I knew it, he had fallen to the ground, and it was time for me to enjoy my vacation.

"Haha, Asshole.... That's what you get." I slid my shades on, walked to collect my luggage, and went to find my driver. I saw him holding up the sign with "King" and I walked over to him.

"Hello, I'm Mrs. King."

"Welcome to Italy, ma'am. Please follow me this way." I followed him to the SUV and hopped in as he put my luggage in the back. I was wowed as we pulled out of the airport. Italy was beautiful. I decided I might as well enjoy myself since my deed had been done. Shunny booked me at the Anantara Palazzo Naiadi Rome Hotel so I could take full advantage of the amenities, starting with the spa. I got out of the SUV, tipped my driver, and grabbed my luggage. As I walk inside, I always look at my surroundings to make sure no one is tailing me. Hell, you know people never think a black woman should live in luxury.

"Hi, I'm Solice King checking in."

"Welcome to The Anatara Palazzo Naiadi Rome Hotel Mrs. King. You have the penthouse reserved I see. As you are probably aware, we have a pool, spa, gym, bar, and room service amenities. I smiled as they gave me my room cards and walked to the elevator.

Let me call my sister and thank her for this hook-up.

"Hellooooo!"

"Yo baby yo!"

"What up Moe?"

"Shunny shu, I love you, man."

"I love you too Soli So, what did I do?"

"This hotel is AMAZING! Everything is so beautiful. I think you should fly out here."

"No can-do ma'am, I have a date tonight honey."

"Ouuuu saucy, enjoy sis. You deserve it, you work hard for me girl."

"And you know that, sooooo, you may have some extra work to do. I just got word from The League, check your phone."

"Dammit, and I was just about to get a massage. Let me check. Judge Dennis Sonder?"

"Turns out he is a judge that has historically given Black people more time than Whites and has investments in prisons."

"Another scumbag will bite the dust."

"For sure. Get busy honey, he's also the owner of one of the vineyards you have to visit tomorrow. Get your plan together and let me know what you need."

"10-4, I'll hit you back later."

Click.

I'm still going to enjoy the rest of my day, shit. I went to the spa and got the best massage of my life. Jorge rocked my damn world with that massage. I can honestly say, "I got my life" at this spa because it was amazing. I felt so refreshed walking out of there, then boom, I see the asshole I gotta kill. Looks like he is about to go get a happy ending. I guess I should give him one. I saw two of the masseuses talking to one another.

"That guy is so disgusting. What a pig!"

"I cannot believe what he asked you?"

"Hey Ladies, everything okay?"

"Yes, ma'am we're fine. That pig just asked do we give happy endings."

"Oh my, what a pervert. Let him sit there for a while."

"He'll probably get mad and report us if we leave him alone for too long."

"Just tell him you're going to get some supplies or something and take a little break."

"You know what…That is a great idea."

I kept talking to the other one while the blonde went in to tell him they were going to get supplies.

"Thank you! I wish we had guests like you all the time." "It's a woman's world honey. Make them wait on us. By the way, where is your bathroom?"

"It's right down that hall. Have a great stay!"

"Thanks so much!"

As they walk away, I walk in the direction of the bathroom and made sure I checked my surroundings for cameras. I didn't see any, so I went into his massage room. He was face down on the table and he was butt-ass naked. I shake my head. Look at this idiot.

"I heard you wanted a happy ending."

"You heard right, pretty lady."

"We'll just relax, I'm going to give you everything you need."

"I like the sound of that."

I scoff, but if only he knew just how happy his ending was going to be. I grab the warming oil off the table and began to massage his back. Then I straddle his back and kept rubbing with one hand as I pull my blade out with the other. I pull his white hair and whisper into his ear.

"This is for all the black men and women whose life you've ruined."

"Wha…."

I slit his throat. Then I got off him and cleaned my prints off of the bottle. I went and checked out the door to see if the masseuses were coming back. Once I saw the coast was clear, I headed back to my room to shower.

Ringgg, Ringgg, Ringgg.

"What's up sis?"

"X marks the spot."

"Got damn Soli, you did it already?"

"Well, I mean, the opportunity presented itself, Oshun."

"It presented itself, huh?"

"Shunny, haha don't start sis."

"Alright now killer bee. *Buzzzz*! I'll let them know it's done."

"Thank you Oh beautiful one of the Sun."

"Yea. Yea!"

Click.

Ringgg, Ringgg, Ringgg.

"Hey Pops!"

"Hello, my child, how was your flight?"

"Oh, it was great! By the way, what type of grapes did you want me to look into?"

"Sangiovese Grapes. They are in the Chianti region of Italy. Remember we want to get into more restaurants. The Italians love wine from this grape because it pairs well with their dishes. Find a Sommelier there and get their perspective on some more in the area that we could utilize."

"Will do boss."

"Also be safe, they tend to be intimidated by your presence. And what is that sound in the background?"

"Let me go look out the window. Hmm, looks like an ambulance."

"Well, you stay out of their way and enjoy your workcation. Bye love you."

"Love you too Pops."

Looks like they're coming to pick up the trash. I'm sure police will be all over this place soon. Guess I should get dressed, head out for some dinner, and call my husband. We still flirt and carry on like we were newlyweds even though it had already been three years.

Of course, with us getting married in college we had to find a balance and we always found time for one another. Shad graduated a year after we got married and I graduated last year and became the business manager for Waytes Wines.

Mom figured that would be the best way to merge my "two jobs." Shad had been working for an architectural firm in D.C. He drew a plan for our house, and we began building it last month. Everything is so exciting. I never thought I would be so happy. Sometimes happiness doesn't last long.

A year later, my world was shattered when my Aunt Max called to tell us about my Mom's disappearance. I have been finding it hard to cope ever since. All of us have been having a hard time. I remember that call like it was yesterday.

***

Bzzz. Bzzz. Bzzz.

    "Hey Auntie, What's up? Mom's not here"
    "Baby girl, where's your Dad?"

"Ummm, I think he's in the kitchen. Let me go check." "Is your sister there too?"

"Yea, but what's wrong Auntie? You sound weird."

"Soli, please go get your father. It is important."

"Okay, Okay. POPS! Auntie Max is on the phone. It sounds important," I run down the steps.

"I'm in the living room, baby girl, come on in here."

"Hey Max, I'm here, what's up?"

"I need you two to listen to me very closely," I began to get nervous.

"Umm, Umm, I just don't even believe I have to say this. Guys, Angela was in an accident and..."

"WHAT? Maxine, where is she? Is she okay?"

"Brian, please let me finish. They pulled her SUV from the river and were unable to recover her body," My heart sank into my stomach, and I couldn't breathe. Pops' face turns pale as he drops to his knees and lets out a pained yelp. All I could do was stand there.

"No, No, No Aunt Max. There is no way they can't find her. Where is my mommy, Aunty? Where is she?" Shunny walks into the room with Grandma J and they see us in pieces.

"What the hell is going on in here?"

"WHERE IS MY MOMMY, AUNT MAX? Where is she?" I continue to cry out.

"Solice what do you mean where is your mother? Where is my daughter, Max?"

"I'm sorry Mrs. Jean. There was an accident, and they were unable to find her."

"W-W-W-What? Where's Mom?" Shunny begins to cry and runs upstairs.

We were broken. Broken-hearted. Minutes. Hours. Days had gone by and still no word on where Mom was. Aunt Max snuck us Mom's file from work so we could look over what she had to do the day she went missing. Uncle Jack talked to all his contacts at The League. Everything seemed like a dead end.

After a week, we finally had a memorial service for her in her garden. Everyone planted a new flower for her and spoke about her. I was there physically, but mentally, I was anywhere but there. Not even Shad could pull me out of this black hole. Any chance I got, I went back to the crash site and ran scenarios in my head. Even if the crash happened the way they say it did, she would've survived.

I DON'T KNOW YOU

I felt like I had so much going on that I couldn't focus on my marriage anymore, and it was selfish for me to continue to drag him along on my emotional roller coaster. This was the time of year that Mom's mysterious death occurred. It had been 4 years, but it was still fresh for me. Looking for clues about her possible killer and trying to piece together things in her book. Shad and I had been arguing for weeks and I felt there was no light at the end of the tunnel.

"Lice we have to finish this conversation. I'm not going to keep brushing this under the rug."

"Shad, I do not know what you want from me. I am trying."

"It doesn't feel like it. You barely communicate with me anymore and we hardly see each other. Baby, I want kids and every time I bring it up you get defensive. Every time I bring up us spending time together, you tell me how busy your schedule is."

"Baby I'm just not ready. There's so much going on and I…"

"I already know what you're going to say. You said "I" which means your focus isn't on us. Again. I get it. I also know April is a hard month for you because of Ma Angela. But listen, I have a flight to catch I gotta go" He grabs his suitcase and walks out the front door. I just stand there. He was right though. I couldn't tell him that I had been around the world killing people and that I didn't want a child because I hadn't figured out how we could escape a life in The League. I want my kids to have a normal life and not have to deal with this shit.

In our last argument, he told me he felt like he didn't know me. Truth is he only knows a part of me and it's clear that my other life is pouring over into this one. I can't keep blaming Taekwondo and the gym for my bruises and cuts. He's not stupid and he knows when something else is going on.

He's going to be gone for a week to design a building in New York. I have to figure out what I was going to do with my marriage. I love him too much to hold him hostage. I knew what I had to do. It would break his heart if I got killed or if someone tries to hurt him to get to me. I call a divorce attorney. After I hang up the phone my heart drops to my stomach and I began to cry uncontrollably. I drag myself to the shower, slide down to its floor and continue to cry. My heart was in such pain, it felt like I was having a heart attack.

Finally, the shower cut off and I slide the door to the side to crawl out. I grab my robe and go sit in the daybed in our bedroom. I must've sat there for hours because Mina starts to whine and poke me with her nose. "I'm sorry, Love. Mommy is having a rough day. You want to go for a run?" She jumps in a circle happily and went to go get her leash.

I get dressed and took her outside. We began to run through the neighborhood. I just want to keep running. Running from the death of my Mom. Running away from The League. Running away from the family business. Running away from my fears.

We finally made it back to the house and I turned off all my devices and went black. I ordered food to be delivered and I cracked open a bottle of tequila. Once my food was delivered, I sat in the garden with my glass and food. Mina ran around the backyard and played with her toys.

The attorney said he would have the papers delivered to our house by the end of the week. *Sigh*. Killing people didn't feel as bad as this. Me going black must've alerted the whole family because I clearly didn't hear my sister calling my name until she was close to me.

"SOLICE. HELLOOOOO!?", I looked up slowly.

"Hi"

"What the hell is going on? Shad said he has been blowing up your phone and you aren't answering and then I started calling you and you're not answering. The cameras are off. You had us scared to death!" She sits beside me.

"I'm sorry sis. I-I-I-I-I am just tired and out of it today. Do you know? Life is coming hard and fast and I just don't know how to cope right now. I just want to hide." I feel the tears swell in my eyes.

"What the hell is going on? What happened? Talk to me."

"I can't keep doing this sis. I can't protect him. He wants kids like yesterday, and I just can't bring myself to tell him the reason why. I thought I could do this Shunny. I would never forgive myself if something happened to him."

"Whoa Whoa, where is all this coming from? Sis, Rashad loves you more than life. He would understand."

"I don't think he would sis. I gotta divorce him to protect him. That's the only way."

"DIVORCE? That man is the love of your life. That's going to make both of yall suffer."

"It's the only way Shunny."

"Maybe you should talk to Pops." I begin shaking my head from side to side.

"I'm not like Mom. She had it all but I'm not sure that I can. Now, look at us and Pops. Grieving her loss for the last 4 years."

She just hugged me and let me cry. Shunny stayed the night with me and assured Shad I was okay. Being the man that he is, he finished his work early and made it home a couple of days early. I was still a mess, even with Shunny being there the last few days. "I'm home Lice", he walked through the door, and I could tell he had been stressing, too.

"Hey, Bro, I'm going to head out. You two talk." I lifted my head from her lap and sat up.

"Thanks, sis. Love you", He hugged her as she walked out the door then directed his attention to me. "Baby, what's going on?" Unfortunately, there was a knock at the door from the mail service. He looked at the envelope and then back at me.

"Lice, what is this?" I could tell he was confused because he knew the attorney's name from TV and that he handled divorces.

"Umm, Uh, we need to talk Rashad." I looked away from him.

"Why are you getting mail from Darren Townes Law Offices?" I felt him glaring at me in confusion.

"Shad I think we need to end our marriage. We're not happy and you want something I cannot give you at the moment. You deserve happiness and I…"

"From the day I met you, you've been my happiness, Solice. This ain't the answer baby. All it takes is work. We can work through anything!"

"Rashad, I can't do this anymore. I want a-a-a divorce!"

"Yo, you can't be fucking serious. Solice, don't do this shit man. What are you running from?"

"I can't let my selfishness affect your happiness. I can't and I won't drag you down with me. I love you too much."

"Man, this shit ain't love. Love is work. You show up every day for love. This shit that you're talking about right now is bogus," He threw the package on the floor and went upstairs.

I just sat there feeling lower than trash. Then I heard him coming back down the stairs and stopping to look at me.

"Tell me this is what you want and there's nothing I can do to change your mind."

I took a deep breath and the tears started to roll down my face.

"Solice I'm never going to make you feel trapped. This shit hurts yo. We have been through too much, but if this is what you want, I'll sign the papers and you can have it all."

I nodded because I couldn't even get the words out of my mouth again. He scoffed and grabbed the package off the floor and started to sign as tears ran down his face. Without a word, he went upstairs and packed some clothes. He came back down and kissed me on the forehead then kissed Mina's head.

He left. I fell on the floor gasping for air and began rocking myself. I couldn't believe what I had just done to my baby. I prayed that this wouldn't turn his heart to stone. I asked the ancestors to look over him.

For the next few months, I began therapy again. I hadn't seen Shad since he left the house that day. His attorney would always do the appearances and since he said I could have everything it wasn't a messy divorce. But I did what any other remorseful and disgruntled ex-wife would do. Stalk his social media. Ride past places he's normally at. And there was nothing. Hell, even his parents stopped talking to me for a while.

I had fucked up, but my honesty would be even more fucked up. My therapist told me to stop looking for him after all these months. If we were meant to be, even if it was just to be friends, we would find our way back to one another, but he needs to do his own healing. I knew I could've found him if I wanted to, but I had to be a big girl and respect his space since I'm the one who broke his heart.

Luckily, my assignments from both The League and Waytes Wines had cooled down. They picked a mighty fine time to chill after my divorce. I guess they figured I wasn't in the right state of mind to continue. I know I needed a vacation, so I took a trip to Virginia Beach. Nothing fancy, but enough tourism for me to have a little fun. I invited Shunny and my cousin Zara, but they both had midterms.

Even Destiny and Lena were busy, so a solo trip with Mina it was. I packed our stuff up and got on the road. The beach was always a safe space for me to think and relax. I put on my breakup playlist and sang my heart out.

"Unbreak my heartttttt, say you love me againnnn" After Toni it was Monica.

"You should've known better than to think I would leave! You should've known better than to doubt meeeeeee!" Then it was Solange.

"I TRIED TO LET GO MY LOVERRRRR, THOUGHT THAT IF I WAS ALONE THEN I COULD RECOVERRRRR, TO WRITE IT AWAYYYYY OR

95

CRY IT AWAYYYY AWAY AWAAYYYYYY"

Every sad song had its own ugly cry and by the time I made it to the beach villa, I was exhausted.
We got inside and I fed Mina then went running myself a bath. I figured it would be easier for me to order in, so I called in an order to a vegan restaurant because I needed a change in eatery. I pulled out a bottle of our rosé, stripped, and slid into the tub.

I sat there and drank out of the bottle because who needs a glass anyway. I told my phone to play Whitney Houston, "I Believe in You and Me," and I let the tears fall down my cheek. I think about everything that had happened in my life over the last couple of years. It was borderline unbelievable. I had lost my mom and husband. These were two of the most important people in my life. I'm not even sure that I am present. Sometimes I just feel like I am on autopilot.

I guess I should consider dating. At least that would give me something to do other than work. The pickings look kind of slim from what I've seen so far. There's only one fish in the sea for me. Mina is barking. I should get out of this tub so I can eat and go to bed. Hmm, maybe I should go for a walk on the beach with Mina first.

The moon is beautiful, and I just feel like being in her light. I throw on a nightgown, grab Mina's leash and walk out the back door, and down the path to the beach. As soon as her paws touch the sand, she breaks from me and runs down the damn beach. I can't believe this girl. I run behind her as she comes to a sudden stop at a stranger.

"I'm so sorry. I don't know what got into her. She normally…"

"It's okay Solice" I knew the voice and all the hairs on the back of my neck and arms stood up. I couldn't even move. I began having a panic attack. Shit, if I was on a mission, I would be good as dead. At the rate my heart was beating, I was going to have a heart attack.

Before I knew it, I had blacked out and woke up on a couch with Mina sitting in front of me. *Damn.* Where is my gun? I knew this shit had to be a dream because there ain't no way. Maybe, I'm dead. That's it. I'm dead. I saw a shadow coming down the hallway. My eyes were still blurry. Well here comes the grim reaper coming to take me.

"Are you okay?"

"Am I dead?"

"Lice, come on man. Are you okay?" He kneeled in front of me.

"I haven't heard you call me that in a long time. But yes, I'm okay. What are you doing here, Rashad?" He was still fine.

"I needed to get a break away from the city and away from traveling. What are *YOU* doing here?"

"Honestly?"

"Yea, be honest."

"I've been taking our divorce kinda hard. I've just been having a hard time finding myself, especially with you gone and losing mom. I want to apologize to you for making an irrational decision. I didn't consider your feelings. I was only thinking of myself. That was wrong." He stared at me for a second.

"I didn't fight for you, Lice. I acted out of hurt and I apologize for that. We had been going through it for weeks, and maybe I backed you into a corner."

"No, No, this was all on me. I bottled everything up and I doubted your ability to understand." He nods.

"I will always be here for you, Lice. And I mean always. I have taken time to process what happened, and I know with us beefing you didn't feel heard or seen, maybe."

"I'm just glad we could finally have a conversation. I know this has been rough on the both of us, but I am hoping that one day we could be close again."

"Yeah, I'm glad we got to talk, too. I have to admit I was tempted to leave you passed out on the beach. You started freaking out and shit," we both laugh.

"SHAD! You know damn well you wouldn't leave me out there. Mina would've dragged me behind you."

"Haha, yea you're right. I miss my girls. I mean Mina," I smiled because although I know he said Mina, I know he misses the both of us and I appreciated that because Lord knows I miss him.

"I'm going out to get some dinner. Do you want to come?"

"Yea, I'll roll with you. What do you have in mind?"

"Sushi."

"Heavy on the sake, though."

"Haha, boy come on here. You're a lush."
We finished the weekend hanging out before I had to go on another mission on Monday. He took Mina home with him and checked on the house for me. I was glad that I had gotten my best friend back and I began to feel like myself again.

STRAIGHT SHOOTER

Before I head out on my missions, I always have to do an inventory of what weapons I need to carry with me. My around-the-way girl, which is what I called my Springfield 9MM Hellcat, travels everywhere with me. Her husband, Mr. Ruger-57 isn't far behind her because you know, run up get done up. I think I'll take my SIG MCX Rattler as well. My Imperial Wakizashi sword is always a must, along with my Black Ronin Shuriken throwing stars. Love my throwing stars. They're a Solice favorite. The 4 razor-edged blades that are hella easy to conceal.

I'm a simple assassin. I don't need too much outside of my hands and select weapons, I'm straight. As I close my weapons locker room, I always make sure I grab my crystals. You always need extra protection by way of the Divine. I threw my duffle bag in the trunk and went back in the house to take Mina for our morning run.

"Mina! Come on, mama. Let's go!"

She always runs out of the house like a bat out of hell. You'll never meet a goofier but highly trained Doberman in your life. I put her on the leash, and we headed out of the gate for our run. I had to mentally prepare myself for this trip. Everything is strategy. I have to coordinate with Shunny and Uncle Jack.

"Hey Siri, Call Shunny." As the phone rang, I ran through my checklist in my head.

"DJ, please, pick up your phone, I'm on the request line!"

"If it's worth it, then let me work it, I put my thang down flip it, and reverse it."

"It's his if he can get it wet! Oww oww"

"T.M.I. ma'am!"

"Haha, what's up, sis?"

"Nothing much, going over some specs in my head about the trip tomorrow."

"Don't worry, your passport, travel arrangements, and business meetings have all been taken care of."

"Did you send over the stuff on Mr. Slade Walker?"

"Absolutely, he's staying at the same hotel as you, so it should be pretty easy. Dress sexy, girl."

"Eww why? I haven't had a chance to look over everything yet."

"Well love, he is a known sex trafficker in Hollywood, specifically of Black women, boys, and girls."

"You're fucking kidding, right? What a damn sicko."

"Unfortunately, and he's basically like old boy with the 'I like ya, and I want ya, now we can do this easy way or the hard way' type of vibe."

"So, I gotta torture his ass huh? I have to get the locations of where he is keeping them."

"Absolutely, but no worries, I'm coming with you!"

"Thank God, I know his ass is sneaky."

"Yep, and Unc is coming, too."

"Heavenly Ancestors, you know Unc can blow a low profile."

"Definitely, butttt he can also POP a motherfucker, if need be."

"And on that note, I am getting off the phone."
Click.

That child is crazy as hell. I think me and Mina need some sanity before we leave tomorrow.

"Mina, do you wanna go see Pop Pop?"
She barked happily and we made our way back to the house. As we were walking down the block, I felt like we were being followed. Just my luck, we were being followed by a cop. He finally decided he was going to pull up beside me.

"Excuse me Miss, are you from this area?"

"Yes, I live down there. Is there a problem, Officer?"

"I've never seen you around here before."

"Me and my dog jog around the neighborhood all the time. Have I done anything wrong? She's on a leash." He scoffed and nodded to me as he drove off. I remember his license plate, so I was going to get his ass later for that bull he just pulled. There's nothing I love more than getting trash off the streets.

I finally got in the house and finished packing my clothes. I grabbed Mina's favorite blanket, and we got in the car, pulled out of the garage, and locked the house down.

"Hey Shelby, play N.W.A. – Fuck the Police" I sped out of the driveway and headed towards the interstate to my parent's house. It was such a pretty day despite my encounter with the police. Pulling into my parent's driveway, I see Pops outside power washing the house.

"Pops! What are you doing sir?"

"Hey baby! Hey Mina!"
Mina hopped on him in excitement.

"How's Pop Pop's granddog? You want Pop Pop to fix you a steak tonight, don't you?"

"That's why she's spoiled now."

"Well, you haven't given me any two-legged grandbabies yet so I guess I will spoil who I have right now, isn't that right Mina?"

"Hmmm. A steak does sound nice."

"Shoot, I know it does. Let's go get the grill started Mina."

"Is Shunny coming over?"

"I hope not for dinner. You know she's a 'vegan' and doesn't want her food touching meat."

"Great Ancestors, Pop you're going to have to let that go. Haha, she is true to it. I tried it for a couple of months, and it wasn't that bad.

"I'm a carnivore baby girl. Anyway, here's a plate. I know you got a flight to catch. It's nice to have my kids taking over the business. I did all that traveling all over the world when I was young. It's your turn now and bring some good business in while you're doing it."

"Yes, sir! Thanks for the opportunity, Pops. I love you and I'll see you when I get back."

"Love you too baby girl. Be safe."

I took my plate and hopped back in the car to head to Dulles. But before I did, I had Shunny pull up everything on that cop. Turns out he was a serial cheater and a racist. She leaked all his cheating rendezvous and his body cam footage to local news stations and internal affairs. That should keep him busy for a while.

Once I arrived, I sat in the car and ate my food, while trying to strategize about how to handle this next hit. It was risky, but nothing that I couldn't figure out. I grabbed my bags out of the trunk and walked into the departure terminal to check-in. I'm glad they have our tickets saved in our phones now because I definitely would've lost it. As I walked through the priority security check, I thought I saw a familiar face as I squinted my eyes to look.

"Dre? Dre McCargo?"

"Long time no see sis!"

Dre is Shad's best friend, but he is also in the CIA. I had to watch how I moved around him because I knew he would observe everything.

"Where are you headed?"

"The Waytes Wine business has me headed to the California Wine Festival. Pops wants me to explore some new ventures while I'm out there."

"Oh, yea? I'm headed to Cali myself. My brother is getting married. By the way, how is Shad? I haven't spoken to him in a while."

"Uhhh, I haven't spoken to him since last week when he brought Mina back. You know when he has a big project he goes M.I.A."

"That's for sure. Well, if you talk to him before I do, please tell him to check in."

"Will do! What part of California are you headed to?"

"I'll be in San Diego for the weekend. How about you?"

"I'll be in Santa Barbara for a couple of days and probably ride out to L.A."

"Bet! Be safe sis. I'll catch you later."

Shit, I'm glad that's over. I always felt like I was under surveillance around Dre, even though he is Shad's best friend. I trust a CIA agent just as much as I trust the FBI, which is not at all, family or not. I stopped and grabbed a bottle of water on the way to my terminal then found a seat near the window. I loved to watch the planes take off. It always brought peace to me. I put my earbuds in and turned on my meditation music to get ready for my flight.

"We are now servicing our Priority Class members", I heard the flight team's announcement over my music. Of course, this is my favorite part of flying. Whew child, the dirty looks I get when I walk over to the priority line with Jordans and a Nike yoga suit on. Let's not even discuss the flawless braid-out. They don't even know how to act. I heard one Karen say, "What does she do?" Bitch, I'm a boss and you wish you could do what I do.

"Hello, Mrs. King, thank you for flying with us today."

"Thank you for having me, Monica."

I looked back and smiled at Karen as I walked through the entrance. Caring what people think about me has never been my M.O. If I am comfortable with myself, there ain't one opinion in the world that I care about. I gave the flight attendant my bags and went to take my seat. I slid my shades on and turned my music up as I got comfortable. I always check my surroundings before I close my eyes. By the time everyone is seated and ready for takeoff, I am already asleep.

"This is your pilot speaking. Welcome to beautiful and sunny California."
Damn, I can't believe I slept the whole 6-hour flight.
I'm glad we made it safely, but now it's go time. I have a 48-hour window to take out Slade. We're in the same hotel so it shouldn't be hard, but I know I have to get through security. I need to call my homegirl Tay while I'm out here, maybe we can catch up while I'm out here. Anyway, let me stay focused.

I get up from my seat and walk to the exit. I went to go find my bags and look for my driver. It's always a pleasure to be treated like royalty and nobody knows who you are. I waved to my driver, he took my bags, and I followed him to the car.

Santa Barbara wasn't bad, I could get some shopping done. A girl must look her best. The Santa Barbara harbor is beautiful, and my hotel is within walking distance of the boardwalk. My driver stops in front of my hotel to let me out and carried my bags inside. I tipped him and got settled in. I had to make sure I logged into my computer securely so that I could access the file on Slade.

The tracking system allowed me to tap into the location settings on his phone and mirror his location to my phone. He appeared to be having lunch at a nearby Spanish restaurant, that's right up my alley. First, I'm going to change into something more "Santa Barbara" appropriate.

A bikini with a skirt or a maxi dress? Since Mr. Walker is 'Mr. Sex Trafficker' I guess less is more would be the best logic. I threw on the bikini and tied on the wrap skirt. "Hmmm...Stilettos or no stilettos? Stilettos and red bottoms for the bourgeois folks here in Santa Barbara." I slid on my lime green Christian Louboutin to match my lime green bikini set. With a little mascara, lip gloss, a hair tussle, and my .22 strapped to my thigh, then I am ready to head out. As I walked past the mirror, I had to compliment myself.

"Damn! I look good, haha."

I grabbed my wrist wallet and headed out of the door. Standing by the elevator I could feel eyes looking at me, but hell who wouldn't want to look at one of god's

107

greatest creations? I walked into the elevator and laughed to myself. I knew once I got to the first floor, I had to give them the "she makes me weak at the knees" walk.

Soon as the door opened, I stepped into my role and sashayed my ass right through that lobby like I was on the runway at New York Fashion Week. Baby the whispers by women and gawking by men was the funniest thing ever. I've never been an attention whore but this time, I needed all the attention I could get so that scumbag Slade could fall right into my trap.

Once outside, I looked over to my left to see how far the restaurant was. It was only a block away, so it wasn't a bad distance to strut my stuff. Hell, if Mariah Carey could run in heels on a treadmill, I knew I would be fine. On my walk, I checked in with Shunny and Unc to let them know where I am.

Unc couldn't make it, but he made sure his son, Tobin, would cover me while in Cali, at least until Shunny got there. All my specs were sent over to Tobin and I was ready to rock as soon as I spotted Slade sitting on the patio outside enjoying a meal with some other men. That's fine. I was hungry anyway.

My main goal coming here was to pique their interest in me. I asked the waitress to be seated on the patio as well so that they could get a better look and so could I. I looked over the menu for a bit and decided on fajitas and water. This patio had an awesome view of the water, so I just gazed at the water until the waitress came back with a random margarita.

"Here you are señora, from the gentleman in the red blazer." I had to scoff because he was so predictable.

"Hi, I don't drink. Sorry. Tell him that it was very kind of him." I lied my ass off. I chug margaritas like a white boy at a Frat party. I would have to let this one slide though.

"Okay Ma'am, I will let the gentleman know. He walked over to Slade to inform him that I had turned down his drink. The audacity of that asshole to smile at me when glanced back at his table. He leaned over to speak.

"You're a beautiful woman!"

"Yes, I know. Thank you"

I turned back around and greeted the server bringing out my food. The food looked amazing. I began to eat, and this prick invited himself over to my table. I guess a perv can't help but to be a perv.

"My name is Slade Walker, and you are?"

"Revyn Frost."

"Revyn Frost? What a beautiful name to match such a beautiful woman.

"So, I've heard." I respond dryly.

"What brings you to Santa Barbara?"

"I love the beach. And you?"

"I love the company of a beautiful woman and wine."

"Well lucky you. I've heard Santa Barbara has a great wine festival?"

"Yes, yes. You should let me show you around."

"What about your friends over there?"

"Oh, they will be fine. Please finish eating and I will see them off."

"Well alright."

I finish eating my food and the server informs me that Slade the Perv has paid for my meal. I walk to the restroom to make sure my tracker is still securely under my boob. As soon as I walk out of the restroom, these fools grab me, throw a bag over my head, and haul me off to the back of a van. I laugh to myself because they were practically doing my work for me. They are sloppy as hell. No zip ties, handcuffs, nothing. I guess they figure most of their victims are so petrified that they don't fight back. Wrong bitch. I snatch that bag off my head and pull my gun from under my skirt.

The van finally stops, and I am sitting there waiting for their asses to open those back doors. The doors fly open and there is Tobin.

"Tobin! What the hell?"

"Sorry Cuz, your location started moving around at top speed so there was no way we were going to let them take you far."

"Aww man, I wanted to bust a cap in their asses. So where are we?"

"Looks like we're at a safe house or a hideaway of some sort. We took the cameras out before we took these guys out so let's go inside and see what we can find."

"Alright, well let me throw this bag back on and you all drag me inside."

"Let's do it."

My cousin hauls me inside. I feel them carry me up the steps and walk to a room. Slade didn't know any better, hell he didn't know half of the men that worked for him. Tobin sits me down in a chair and pulls the bag off my head. I smile at Slade.

"Funny seeing you here pervo."

"Excuse me?"

"I said, Funny seeing…" He lunges at me.

"You black bit…"

Before he knew it, I had drawn my gun to his face.

"Oh Slade, what were you about to say? I can't hear you, you fucking prick. A guy once called my mom a Black Bitch and she tortured him for it." I stand up and kick him in the chest. I smile at him again.

"Now, Mr. Walker, you're going to tell me and my friends here where you're hiding all of those people that you have stolen and forced into the sex trade."

"I'm not telling you shit, you stupid bitc…" I pressed my .22 to his temple.

"Mr. Walker. Watch your tone.   Is this your personal phone and laptop?"

"Keep your grimy hands off of my things!"

"Here, Tob. I guess if the perv doesn't want to tell us we'll just have to kill him and find out on our own. It's not like we don't have the resources to destroy him. What's your choice of death, Mr. Walker? Poison made to look like a natural cause of death, or a gunshot wound to the head? Quick and easy."

"Okay, Okay, Don't kill me and I'll tell you what you need to know. Some girls are in the bottom of this house, below the basement. Others have already been sold and some are on an undisclosed shore island next to St. Croix." I suck my teeth and look at him.

"How do we know you aren't lying? Take us downstairs."

One of Tobin's boys pulls him up from his chair and pushes him towards the door with a shotgun to his back.

"Watch him, he's a slick motherfucker that would try to throw himself down the steps."

"Got you, boss" he nods to Tobin and walks out the door.

"We need to get Shunny on the phone so she can hack into his devices to see what she can find."

"You know I know a little something, something too cuz."

"I'm sure you do! Here, Shunny uses this USB extender fob to log her into any device, and with his iPhone and Macbook
having connected profiles, we can find anything."
I hand it over to him.

"I'm going to get Shunny on the phone."

"Yello!"

"What's up sis, we need you to look into some information."

"Are you all plugged in with USB?"

"Tob just plugged in."

"TOBIIIIII, what's up fool? What are you doing there?"

"UHHHH Oshun, we are in the middle of a mission. You and Tob can catch up after we get this info."

"Such a Debra Downer. Anyway, let me grab my laptop. What exactly are we looking for?"

"Pervo said that he has them located here in his compound, an undisclosed island near St. Croix and that he has already sold some of the women. I need a ledger for buyers and confirmed locations for women sold on the island."

"Say less."

"Less is said."

"Don't start sis, I'm trying to work here."

"Work your magic."

"Found it. I'll send everything to you and Tobin's phone."

"Thank you, ma'am."

"I also grabbed all of Pervy Slade's info from his phone and laptop so you can leave that there and get out of there. Looks like he has some cops on the payroll who work his security."

"10-4 sis, we're out."

Tobin and I wipe our prints down from everything we touched then head down to the basement.

"Well Mr. Walker, it seems as if you aren't a liar. Not today anyway."

"Yes, so please release me."

"Oh yes, I'm going to release your evil soul from your body." I shot him in the dick. Serves him right. He screams like a little bitch, and it was quite amusing.

"Keep him alive until we find the rest of the people. Then we'll come back to finish pervo." I leave the basement and look around the house to see if I could find anything else in the house. After some digging, I found mortgage documents on different properties around the States, but none of them were under Walker's name. I took pictures and sent them to The League and Shunny. My phone began to ring.

"Yo!"

"We got live feeds and locations of the people."

"Good. Kill him."

"10-4"

I waited for Tobin and his men to finish cleaning up Walker's spot, and then we left. They dropped me back off at my hotel. Once I got back to my room I showered and got a drink of tequila from the minibar. This particular hit bothered me because as easily as they snatched me up, I can only imagine how they did other unsuspecting women and girls. I laid down to sleep because I still had to do Waytes Wines business in the morning.

Drinnnn Drinnnn Drinnnn

Damn alarm clock. Guess it's time for me to get up and go meet some restaurateurs. I grabbed my fitted, turquoise suit out of my garment bag and threw on my peacock-inspired Steve Madden stilettos. I looked in the mirror and slicked my hair up in a bun. I never needed much makeup, so I added a light touch of foundation, mascara, and a wine-colored lip gloss. It was game time.

"Let's make Waytes Wines some money."

I pop my collar, look in the mirror, and walk out of the door.

IT'S RAINING BLOOD

I am exhausted. I have been to wine festivals non-stop for the last two months. Brian has me working overtime. The Spring months leading into summer are our busiest times. We have to secure new businesses and are experimenting with new grapes. Pops just purchased a new vineyard in California so me and Shunny have been bouncing around from coast to coast. Mina has been spending most of her time with Rashad and I miss them both. We call and check in every other week but it's not enough. This shit gets lonely.

Buzzz Buzzz Buzzz.

My phone started to go off.
     "Hello"
     "Hi, Solice King? This is Anderson Benito."
     "Yes, Mr. Benito, How are you?"

"I am doing well. I wanted to let you know that we have accepted your father's proposal for building our restaurant on the new vineyard."

"Excellent. I will be sure to let him know. Thank you for your business."

"I heard you're in Cali for a little while."

"Now where did you hear that?"

"You can't come to Cali and do business without me knowing Mrs. King."

"It's actually Miss King, but I'll keep that in mind."

"Have dinner with me."

"Hmmm, I don't know. I'm kind of busy."

"If it's only Miss King, then you're not that busy."

"Touché', where do you suggest we meet?"

"Meet me at my Newport Beach restaurant around 10 pm. Wear something sexy."

"What else would I wear?"

"You could wear nothing."

"Haha, cute Mr. Benito. I will see you at 10 pm."

"Ciao."

Mr. Benito was fine! Not finer than my ex-husband but damn close. He was Cuban and Black and raised in Long Beach, California. He had jet-black, deep waves and a salt and pepper beard. He was about 6'6 with juicy, pink lips, dimples, and beautiful, smooth, sunkissed caramel skin. Chile, he was bow-legged too. A fine work of art. Mmm Mmm mmm.... I met Mr. Benito at a wine festival about a year ago.

I guess meeting fine men on the job seems to be my thing. He was looking for a wine company to be the primary vendor for his restaurant. I saw him carrying a hot-cold bag on the back of his bike but since he looked like a delivery guy, I never thought he would stop at my table. We caught eyes and he stopped.

"Hey Miss, what do you have here?"

"Hello Mister, I am Solice and these are our Waytes Wine Trio. The Trio consists of Rosé, Prosecco, and Moscato. I also have our special Cabernet Sauvignon and Pinot Gris."

"Solice? That's beautiful. You're beautiful too and so are these bottles."

"Thank you, Mister...?"

"Oh sorry, Anderson. Anderson Benito. I own Benito's Cuban Bistro up the block. I was looking for some wine pairings with my two signature dishes. The Fricase de Pollo and Ropa Vieja."

"Well, those sound good. What are they?"

"I'm glad you asked," he flashes that million-dollar smile, and my body starts to react. *What the hell?* He reaches in the hot-cold bag and pulls out two small mason jars then a fork.

"This first one is the Ropa Vieja. Here taste." He held the folk to my lips and without resistance I took a bite because it smelled so damn good. *DAMN!* It tasted even better. The food must have drugs in it because I forgot he was standing in there. I was lost in a moment in time.

"Damn, I hope I get that reaction from everyone who tries it. I haven't heard a moan like that in a while." I know I turned red. He smiles again and she starts to react again. I know it's been a while but *JESUS!*

"Now try the Fricase de Pollo," I take another bite. *Good Lord!* I wanted to take my panties off and throw them at him.

"Good right?"

"Yessss, this is *AMAZING*! Where did you learn to cook like this?"

"My Papi used to throw down in the kitchen and he taught me everything he knows. He was a cook before he left Miami."

"So, you're from Miami?"

"Nah, Papi is from Cuba and swam to the U.S. with my grandparents when he was a little dude. When he turned 18, he was sick of Miami and moved across the country to Long Beach where he met the daughter of a Black Panther. Haha, he told me her afro caught his attention, along with her brown sugar complexion and loud voice. He was a cook in the cafeteria on her college campus and saw her at a rally one day after his shift.

Papi said he was curious, so he asked her what she was protesting about and after she explained to him about the Panthers and her cause, all he wanted to do was learn more about her world and how to be a part of it. He enrolled in school to be a history teacher because he figured that would be the greatest way to effect change in our communities. Now they both are professors at the university they graduated from."

"Wow, that's so dope."

He took his phone out and showed me his parents.

"No wonder you're so fine. Your parents are gorgeous."

"So, I'm fine huh?"

"You're alright."

"I'll take that from you, Ms. Solice. Now tell me a little bit more about your wines."

"Well based on the meats and flavors of your meals, I think you should go with the special Cabernet Sauvignon and Pinot Gris." I poured him a sample of each. He closed his eyes as he sampled both.

"Good choice. I like these. How soon could you get me a few cases of each?"

"As soon as I call my Pops."

"You're Pops? Family-owned business huh?"

"Absolutely!"

"I think I am going to like this partnership," he said as he grabbed my hand and kissed it.

"Here, take my information and send me over your contract." I took his card.

"Just like that?"

"I've tasted everything I needed to make a decision. Almost everything." He smiled at me then continued his bike ride. This was going to be the start of a wild and fun business relationship. We kept in contact for a while and eventually the opportunity presented itself for us to link on business. Pops liked his restaurant, and he liked Pops style and how he ran his business. They talked often after I introduced him, which is why I don't understand why he decided to share the good news with me. Well, I know why Mr. Benito is quite smitten with me and I can't blame him. I guess let me call Pops and tell him the good news.

"Hey, Babygirl!"

"Hey, Pops! I wanted to congratulate you on another successful business deal."

"Thank you! Anderson called me not too long ago to let me know."

"Oh, he did, did he?"

"Yes, he did. Why don't you go check out his Newport Beach restaurant?"

"I think I will. Catch you later Pops. I love you, old guy!"

"Love you too, Soli. Be safe!"

Tobin and Shunny had been working on a couple of projects in the Los Angeles area, so I guess I will take a ride to see them today. Ain't no fun if the crew can't get none. I pack a day bag and ride up to L.A. to hang with my partners in crime. Tobin runs a security company as his primary means of income and Shunny works on the logistics and distribution for Waytes Wines. They both were in the zone when I walk through the door.

"Is D.C. in the houseeee? Is L.A. in the houseeeee?"

"Solice don't come into my house with all that noise. See, that's why we left you in Anaheim!"

"Tob, you need to lighten up. All y'all do is work, work, work. We are in our prime!"

"All we do is work, work, work? Says the assassin that travels around the world killing people. Now isn't that the damn pot calling the kettle black."

"We are in L.A., and when in L.A., we do what L.A. does."

Shunny comes from the kitchen, eating like always.

"And what's that, sis?"

"Party and bull-ish and party and bull-ish"

They look at each other and laugh. Then they look at me like I'm crazy.

"My darling sister, you must haven't seen your new list." Shunny smirks.

"Check your phone."

"Y'all sure know how to ruin a good time, honey."

I looked at my phone and saw that The League had sent me a whole damn list of people on the West Coast to get.

"Where the hell did all of this come from?!"

"Well, while you had downtime with Waytes Wines, they thought you would have a little more time to get some other things done."

"Shunny, are you serious?" I look at her and frown.

"As a heart attack girl, you better get on your specs!"

I drag my laptop and my phone out to finish checking my specs. It appears that I have my work cut out for me. We sit and rap about strategy for a while and get some takeout. When I check the time, it ended up being 9 pm.

"Oh shit! I gotta go yall!"

"Where are you going?"

"I got a hot date like you should get, sis."

"Hot date? Rashad flew out here to take you on a date?"

"NO RASHAD DID NOT FLY OUT HERE TO TAKE ME ON A DATE!"

"Well, who the hell are you going out on a hot date with, Solice."

"If you may know Tobin, his name is Anderson."

"Anderson? Is he white?"

"No, fool, he's not white, is he Shunny?"

"Naw he's not white but he's damn fine, OKAY!" I slap my sister five.

"Here yall go. Does my cousin-in-law know you're going out on this "hot date?"

"Tobi, whose cousin are you? Mine or Rashad's?"

"That's always going to be my boy."

"Yeah, Yeah! I'm going to take a shower and get dressed."

I walk upstairs to the bathroom and hop in the shower. As I wash off, I think about how Shad would feel. I also thought about how we had been divorced for the last 3 years and I hadn't been on a date in years let alone allowed someone to touch me. Most of my time was consumed with work, unfortunately. I knew he was dating so it was time for me to get back on the wagon. I sigh and shake my head because it sucks. I couldn't be mad though because I was the idiot that filed for divorce.
Oh, well. The past is the past.

I figured a wash-and-go would be the easiest thing for me to do to my hair. I hop out of the shower and dry off. I slide my emerald, green ribbed tank top dress on and grab my strappy sandals. Time is ticking so I grab my stuff and head back downstairs.

"See y'all later!"

"Be safe!", they collectively yell from the living room. I hop in the car and head to Newport Beach for my "date." When I pull up to Anderson's restaurant, it is packed outside. On the weekends it turns into a lounge slash bar. I pull up to the valet and get out to walk to the front door.

"Name, please."

"Solice King."

"No Solice King on the list ma'am."

"Solice Waytes?"

"No Solice Waytes either. You'll have to get in line."

"Who? I'll leave before I wait in this damn line after I was invited here." The security guard saw I wasn't having it, so he radioed into the other security inside.

"Miss King, are you out here making a scene outside of my restaurant? That's not even your style, mami." I look up at the balcony and there he is smiling at me.

"Mr. Benito, do not play with me."

"Let her up, Malcolm."

He let me inside, and I walk upstairs to the balcony where Anderson is. There he was waiting with a drink in hand and having the time of his life. There was such freedom about him. As he dances to the reggaeton playing in the background he watches me come toward him.

"You better let your security know who I am next time" I poke him in the chest, and he grabs my hand and kisses it.

"It'll never happen again, Gorgeous. I give my word." Then he spun me around and we began to dance. He began to order tequila shots from the bar, and we drink and dance and drink and dance. Little does he know, tequila makes me horny. No Letting Go by Wayne Wonder began to play, and we started to grind and wind. I felt him growing hard and that shit turned me on even more.

"Anderson, I have to go!"

"Where are you going, baby girl? You just got here." His lips were pressed against my ear.
"I know, but I am lit and I have some work to do."

"Don't bullshit me, Solice. What kind of work do you have to do at 1 in the morning?" He grabs me by the waist and pulls me closer to him.

"Damn it's 1 am already? I gotta get home!"

"Let my driver take you home. It doesn't matter how far it is. She'll make sure you get there safely."

"Alright. Come on."

He holds my hand as we walk down the steps and to the back to meet his driver. I turn around and I see his print through his slacks. I start losing it in my mind. I start smiling and he caught me looking. My silly ass is too drunk to be discreet, but he continues to be a gentleman.

"Alana, please take Miss King wherever she needs."

"Yes, sir."

Before I knew it, I blurt out… "Come with me." Oh hell, why did I say that? I didn't even know if I had put up all my weapons at the villa.

"Okay, I'll come."

He gets into the backseat with me and wraps his arm around me. I felt safe and not too many people outside of my family make me feel this way. I told his driver where to go and we headed back to Anaheim. As I was falling asleep, my hand drops into his lap, and I feel *it*.

That woke me the hell up, and I start to get hot and sweaty. He lifted my chin and kissed me on the lips. I got wet as soon as I kiss him back. I feel his hand go up my dress and he rubs my lips and then my clit. I began to grind my hips as he continues to rub my clit in a circle while we keep kissing.

The partition was already up so Alana couldn't see a thing we were doing. It felt good to be touched. He massages my hard nipples through my dress and then began to nibble on them. I straddle his lap and tongue kiss him as he sucked my nipples. I was taking off his belt when we pull up to my villa. Damn!

I get out of the car and grab his hand. He follows me out of the car, and we keep kissing through the lobby to the elevator. By the time we were in the elevator, he picks my ass up and had me against the wall with my legs wrapped around his waist. Once we got to my door, I slide down to open the door.

I pull him inside the villa and he's grabbing on my ass. He drops his pants to the floor and steps out of his shoes and pants. Anderson comes to pick me up and takes me to the bed. When he lays me on the bed there is a big ass bump there, like a body.

"DAMN, Solice!"

"What the hell? Oshun? ARE YOU IN MY BED? WHY ARE YOU IN MY BED?" This foolish woman turns on the lights.

"SOLICE, is this ANDERSON!? Hello, Mr. Anderson," she says slyly as he covers himself.

"SHUNNY! Get out!"

"Why can't I snuggle with my sister??" She smirks at me like the Grinch.

"Oshun, get out of MY BED"

"Fine, Sister. Nice meeting you Mr. ANDERSONNNN!" She gets up and sashays her ass to the spare bedroom where she should've been in the first place.

"I'm so sorry Anderson." I shake my head and laugh.

"It's ok Miss King, let's lay down."

We lay down with one another and laugh. We talk for a few hours and end up falling asleep. I wake up to Anderson cooking me and Shunny breakfast. She was in there eating like usual. He looked so damn good plating a meal. He had plantain and a Cuban eggs benedict.

"This looks amazing Anderson."

"Thank you mami. Come here, sit."

He serves both me and Shunny then sat and ate with us. We all had a great conversation about life and traveling. After brunch, he calls his ride and kisses me goodbye. When I came back inside, there was my grinning ass sister.

"Did you hit it?" She smiles, standing there with her hands on her hips.

"NO, SHUNNY. You were in my bed and killed the mood."

"It won't meant to be sis, woo woo woo. I just wanted to snuggle with my sissy".

"Oshun, get out of my face. I was young, hot, and ready."

We burst out laughing. I love my sister for it and maybe she was right.

"Alright, now let's get down to business."

"So, your next hit will be Kumar Kupp, the guy that does all of Mom's old boss, Nelson Fuentes's dirty work. When it comes to secretly targeting minorities, especially those in positions of power, he is Fuentes's right-hand man. Apparently, he has arranged for a sniper to be stationed outside of the Grand Prix of Long Beach this Saturday."

"Why the hell would he do that?"

"To blame it on gang violence and continue to make our communities look bad. It's like he gets off on creating violence and uproars in our communities based on his track record. Mom had him as a priority."

127

"Alright, so we have to keep an eye in the sky to make sure we keep the people safe. Call Unc and let them know the type of weapons and tech we need. Also call Emerson to get her tapped in to see if she can get access to street cameras, ATM cameras, stairwells, elevators, etc. Let Tobin know that we need his people on the ground checking out the vantage points with the measuring binoculars so we can make sure our scopes are adjusted properly. Also, check the weather tomorrow to see what type of elements we're going to be shooting in."

Emerson Veda went to school with Shunny to study cyber technology, security, and defense solutions. Not only does she work for the Department of Justice, and has worked for the Marines, she moonlights for us when we have major missions and Shunny can't handle it all. Since this was major and involved plenty of innocent people, I needed all the eyes I could get to make sure this went off smoothly with minimal damage.

"She's in. We have two days to prepare. Get the blueprints for that whole area where the Grand Prix will be held, and I will go for a run around that area."

"Got you! Let's get busy!"

I called Unc to get some equipment and me and Shunny started our planning board. Based on the intel, there may be multiple snipers and or shooters in the area during that time. Most likely they'll be wearing masks and gang colors. We know the Grand Prix is normally a peaceful event.

Saturday morning rolled around, and we were locked and loaded. Everyone was in place. Tobin had his people on the ground. Shunny and Emerson have eyes everywhere while Unc and I were on rooftops with bug drones flying through the sky. The Grand Prix was beginning, and everything remained relatively calm until we spotted our first shooter.

"First shooter has been located. Uncle Jack, you are closest to building B. Please confirm when you have located the target", Emerson radioed in.

"Target has been located."

"Fire!" He shoots.

"Target down, extraction team head to building B to secure the body."

"Targets two and three have been seen. They are on the ground. One has a yellow bandana on walking eastbound toward food vendors and the other is headed southbound in Khakis. Solice are you able to locate them?"

"Yes, I'm following the yellow bandana guy, but it's crowded. I can't take a shot without causing mayhem."

"Tobin, can you secure the guy in khakis?"

"Yes, but he keeps looking at the rooftops, there may be another active shooter."

"Shit! I just picked up the other shooter. Uncle Jack, can you reach building E?"

"I'm out of range Emerson! Someone else has to take him down."

The first shot rang out before we could get to the first shooter. I know I have to act quickly so I grab my scope and turn it to building E to shoot the second shooter then quickly dial back to the ground to find the yellow bandana guy. Just my luck! He's running through the crowd, but I'm following him with my scope. Shit. Shit. Shit. He pulls out a UZI and starts shooting into the crowd. Bullets are flying everywhere, and people are dropping. I have to take this idiot out. Pop! Pop! Pop! I finally knock him off. Tobin shoots the other target and runs to the alley.

"The police are on the scene! We gotta go!", Tobin was yelling through the radio, but I had to be sure that I got all of the shooters. As I was scanning the area, I saw Anderson's food truck shot up. Oh no! I immediately pack my rifle and head down the steps. I quickly slide my rifle into the back of my jeep and run over to Anderson's food truck.

There he is. He seems lifeless from a gunshot wound in the stomach. I check his pulse, and he is still alive but unconscious. His breathing is shallow, and he was turning pale, so I radio Tobin to send one of his people over to help me get him into the jeep.

I speed to the nearest hospital, and they admit him. I had to lie and tell them I was his wife so I could stay with him. The nurses take him to surgery so that they could remove the bullets. After about 3 hours, Anderson was out of surgery but still unconscious. I walk into his room and sit beside him and text everyone where I am.

Anderson was the only man I started to catch feelings for since Shad. I look over at him, hooked to all these machines, and I kick myself for not being able to protect everyone. My job isn't to protect everyone, it's to eliminate the target but the flip side to that is being human and caring about humans.

I sat by his bedside for two days until he woke up.

"Solice...?"

"Hey, A, it's nice of you to join me."

"What the hell happened?" He asks groggily. "How long have I been here?"

"Relax, you were shot at the Grand Prix, and I happened to be in the area when I noticed your food truck. I panicked when I saw it shot up, so I ran in and found you passed out. I brought you here."

"You.... saved my life?" He rubbed his head in so much confusion.

"You can say that, but I'm just happy I could be there for you. Is there anyone that you want to call?"

"Thank you, Solice. Could you please call my sister, Tanya? Tanya's number is 562-987-4567."

"You get some rest, and I will call her."

I smile and rub his hand. He falls back asleep as I call his sister and let her know where he is. When she arrives, she gives me the biggest hug. I'm glad I could stay with him, but it was time for me to get back to business. Kumar Kupp still had to die.

OPEN

"Hey, Baby."

"Hello, Anderson, how are you doing today?"

"Damn, I can't get a 'hey, baby' back?"

"Haha! Anderson, I am working! What can I do for you today, sweetheart?"

"I want to see you. I kind of miss you."

"Anderson, what time is it over there? I know it has to be at least 4 am."

"So? Solice, I want to see you. You've been gone a month."

I was silent because I knew we had been on Kupp's ass for the last month, but he was always heavily guarded.

"Solice, are you still there?"

"Yes, Yes come to D.C., and I'll show you around."

"See that's what I'm talking about! Be spontaneous. Stop being so calculated."

"Whatever, Anderson, BYE!"

132

"Wait, I can stay with you right?"

"I'll think about it. Let me see what Mina says. I told you she doesn't like anyone but her daddy and her Pop pop."

"She'll like me after I cook for her."

"Hahaha don't be trying to bribe my baby."

"Bye, beautiful, I'll see you tomorrow."

"Bye A, see you soon."

What had I gotten myself into? Mixing business with pleasure? I mean his business and company were always a pleasure. I guess I better call the housekeeper to come sooner and get some groceries in the fridge. Instadeliver here I come, and put it in the fridge, please.

I go get in the shower so I can head over to Grandma J's for a briefing because Kupp was turning into one of my hardest targets. I hop out of the shower and get dressed. I grab my phone and book bag then go get in the car to head to Grandma J's house.

I figure I should stop at my favorite coffee house and pick up a latte or something since we're probably going to be at it for a while. As soon as I get out of the car, I see Rashad's black Jeep. I take a deep breath because we hadn't seen each other in a while since we've both been traveling, and he normally will pick Mina up from Pops and vice versa.

I walk into the coffee house and there he was sitting at the table, alone. I got up my nerve to speak and then some tall, lanky chick slid her ass into the booth with him. Oh hell. He saw me. I gave him the 'white man, hello smile' and waved. He then gets up from the booth with the chick and comes to me.

"Hey, Soli, funny seeing you here."

"Ha...ha yes, funny. I was just stopping on my way to Grandma J's house. I see you're out with a friend?"

"Oh yea, that's Kayla."

I nod and look away. He reads my discomfort and then here she comes to make matters more awkward.

"Hey, Shaddy Pooh, who's this?"

Shaddy Pooh? Now, this bitch knows exactly who I am.

"Kayla, this is Solice."

"Solice? Your ex-wifeeeee? Well, HI! Such a pleasure to meet you...finally."

I should shoot her right between the eyes.

"Hi, yes, the one and only. You two enjoy. I think I'm good on the coffee." I chuckle under my breath and walk out of the building, and back to my car. Instead of coffee, I guess I will have to settle for tequila. I stop at the ABC Store, grab a bottle of 1800 and keep going to Grandma J's. As I walk through the door, almost all of my aunts, uncles, and cousins are in attendance. A Friday night cookout?

"What in all the hell is going on in here?" I look at Shunny and Tobin.

"Hey, sis! Grandma J had to bring out the squad."

"Yea, no shit. Hey everyone! Do I smell oxtails?"

I walk to the kitchen to find Grandma J.

"Yes ma'ammmm, what's up cuz? Long time no see?"

"Hey Devin, what did Grandma J have to do to get you out of duty?" Devin is my Mom's youngest sister's son. He's a high rank in The League and a dual agent for an unclassified U.S. organization. I know if Grandma J called him, shit is about to get real. We all eat, drink, and strategize.

I have never in my life heard so much about ballistics, trajectories, velocity, wind speeds, bullet travel rates, etc. By the end of it all, I am exhausted but at least we have a plan. Devin's going to be me and Unc's spotter this time around. We're going to make it look like the CIA ordered this hit on Kupp.

Emerson is handling that piece. As always Tobin is handling the groundwork with some help from his twin Robin. Shunny is securing the locations and visual points within six blocks of where Kupp should be attending a meeting. If that doesn't work, we're going to break into his house and Grandma J is going to poison his ass then we call it a day. When I look at the time, it's 5 am, and Anderson should be arriving at my house in 40 minutes. The great thing is, I'm an hour away.

Buzz Buzz Buzz.

"Hello?"

"Hi Beautiful, I'm here."

"Anderson! What are you doing here already? I'm like 60 minutes away."

"Private Jet. I can wait."

"Somebody is rich," I tease. He laughs.

"No. no need to wait, I can unlock the house from here. I need to shower. I've been at my Grandma's house all night."

"I can make sure you have a great morning after having a long night."

"Don't threaten me with a good time. I'll see you soon!" I bit my lip and did a little shimmy.

"It's a promise."

Click.

I haul ass home. I cannot lie I am excited for our weekend together, especially after seeing Shad out with that broad. As soon as I walk into the front door, I breathe in the most amazing smell, and there are sunflowers everywhere.

"Anderson! What is this?"

"Welcome home, Beautiful!"

"I could get used to this. I haven't been this spoiled in a while. I am impressed."

"I would be happy to make sure you do. Do you want to eat or shower first?"

"Oh, you know I'm not going to let this breakfast get cold."

"A woman who appreciates good food. I am impressed." He smiles at me and begins to feed me eggs and Ropa Vieja. I moan just like I did the first time I tried it.

"How was your flight?"

"It was good. I got some work done and some rest. Still healing and getting better."

"I'm glad to hear that. You look good. You always do". He leans in to kiss me, and I kiss him back. I grab his hand to lead him upstairs to my bedroom. We both laugh as we stand face to face. He lifts my chin to kiss me and slowly begins to remove my clothes. It felt so good to be touched and taken care of after all this time. I begin to take off his clothes and then lead him to the shower.

We kiss again as he runs his fingertips up and down my spine. I grab a sponge and begin to wash his body while he continues to caress my skin. I remember exactly how fine he was from the last time we got this close. Before I know it, he lifts me, wraps my legs around his waist, and pins me against the wall. We keep kissing as I lower myself down on his dick. He bites my neck and puts my hands against the shower wall as I slide up and down.

His tongue trails all over my neck and breasts. As soon as my legs start to quiver from him hitting my spot, he puts me down, bends me over, and slides in from behind. He's grabbing my shoulders and pulling me into each stroke. This man is stroking the hell out of me, and I can't even control my moans or body.

I came and he keeps going. When he stops, I thought he was done but he kneels and throws my legs over his shoulder and began to eat my soul out of my body. He looks up at me and winks. I knew it was going to be a long morning. He has me holding on to the shower head and wall for dear life. I came again, then he laid down in the shower and pulled me on top to ride him.

Mama was tired, but as I said before, I ain't no punk so I rode that man like an equestrian at the Kentucky

137

Derby. And he was so kind to let me cum again before he did. We get up from the floor and wash each other off. Anderson made love to me like he had been waiting all his life to do it. We get out of the shower and dry off so we could lie in the bed.

When he falls asleep, I roll over to check my phone, and here's a message from Shad. What in the hell could he possibly want at 9:00 am? As I open the message, I see, "We need to talk." I always hated his "We need to talk" messages because I never knew what to expect. I figured there was no need for me to respond yet, so I snuggle back up to Anderson and got some rest. His strong arms held me closely and filled my body with warmth. I felt a calm wash over me. I finally felt relaxed.

I wake up and look over at the clock and it's 2 pm. I slept longer than I planned. I slide out of Anderson's arms and write him a note to meet me later and that I have some errands to run. I knew that if I was going to deal with Rashad as a part of my errands, I better get a little sexy just in case his big head girlfriend popped up.

I threw on a long-sleeved, black bodycon dress and some matching black chunky heeled boots. I fluff my hair out in the mirror. I'll do my make-up in the car, so I don't disturb Anderson. I'm sure he'll wonder where I'm going looking like this if he wakes up. I grab my purse and keys then head to the car. I call Shad from the car while doing my makeup.

"Yo!"

"Hey, what's up you said we need to talk."

"Yea, Can you meet me at Mama's office? I'm painting it right now."

"Sure, be there in 20."

"Bet."

My anxiety was through the roof. What if this fool was about to tell me he's going to ask this Kayla broad to marry him and he wants my blessing? We have been cool but not that damn cool. I'd have to slap Shad. Or what if he tells me she's pregnant? Oh, hell no! I was supposed to have his babies.

What if he's moving in with her? Ain't no way Mina is going over there. After asking myself a thousand questions, I finally arrive at Mrs. Rebecca's office. I get out of the car and walk into the office.

"Hellooooo?"

"I'm in here Soli!" He's in the back office and it's crap everywhere.

"Uh, Hey. What's up? You wanted to see me?"

"Thank you for coming. I really want to apologize, Soli. You know I don't get down like that. I will always consider your feelings because our friendship is important to me. Wait...you look good. Like you're glowing." Yes, I had that new dick glow, but he didn't need to know that.

"Oh, really? Thanks, and Thanks for the apology. I apologize for how I acted. I was honestly embarrassed and shocked. I knew you were dating but it caught me off guard a little bit."

"Soli, you never have to be embarrassed when it comes to me. I love you. I would never willingly put you in an awkward situation."

"I know. I love you, too."

He came closer to hug me. I back up a little bit. All the tension in my body left when he hugs and holds me. Lord and he always smells so good. He looks down at me the same way he did when we first hooked up after the wine festival. I am still putty in this man's hand. I couldn't resist so I kiss him. Tongue and all. The same way I did our first night together. I guess I'm always starting some shit. He grabs my ass and keeps kissing me back.

"Shad we gotta stop. We can't do this."

"Soli...I have never. Will never stop loving you. I care about Kayla, but baby, she ain't you. I WILL ALWAYS WAIT FOR YOU! We've been friends and hanging out, so it's only normal that I would want you back." He keeps looking at me.

"Shad I love you more than anything in this world but baby I'm kind of seeing someone too. Do you think we're ready for this?" My baby looks hurt and as much as I like Anderson, I want my husband back more.

"I understand. I think we are. So, what does that mean?" That is such a man's question.

"Well, mine isn't that serious. We've only been involved a couple of months, and he knows I was married. What about Kayla? Haven't y'all been 'dating' for a while?"

"Solice, you're always my first choice. Kayla is cool, but we aren't serious."

"Does she know that? Because if she runs up on me, I'll have to cap her."

"Solice, that ain't funny."

"Shit, I'm not laughing."

"Soli you're not going to shoot anyone", Shit, this negro just doesn't know how fast I'll shoot someone. Especially her.

"Alright. I need some time, Rashad. We'll need to end things with them and seek some couple's therapy." "Deal. Now, can Daddy get a little something, something," I already knew what type of time he was on with that 'little something, something' and it wasn't Maxwell. He has his hands running up and down my backside while pulling me close enough to feel his print.

"Haha, you're Mina's daddy, not mine. And no, you cannot! You probably just slept with that girl this morning. I'm serious about couple's therapy, Shad."
I break his grip then stick my tongue out at him and wave bye.

"Don't stick it out if you're not going to use it!" He says as he's on full attention. I run back to my car and leave.

Well, that was crazy. I got my husband back but I'm about to possibly hurt a man who I've grown to care about. If it ain't one thing it's another. I went to my storage garage to switch my car out for my motorcycle and headed to meet up with the team. It was about 4 pm when I made it to the rendezvous point.

I hid my bike near the library and then walked into the warehouse two blocks from Kupp's meeting spot. Kupp was scheduled to leave his meeting at 5 pm, so we had to be in our places by 4:30. I walk in, and they start with their shit.

"Where the hell did you come from, Solice?"

"Devin, don't start your mess."

"Damn, she looks like she just got back from a hot date. Doesn't she? Glowing and shit." Uncle Jack chimes in.

"*IF* yall must know, I just talked to my HUSBAND!"

Both of these fools shout in unison, "YOUR HUSBAND?"

"Solice, I know damn well you didn't go off and marry old dude from Cali!" Devin states with confusion.

"Devin, I knew you were crazy, but not this crazy. Rashad, dummy!"

"MY BOY?! But don't you have a visitor?" He raises his eyebrow.

"You're so NOSEY. Shad said he still wants us to be together," I shrug. I go change into my gear.

I grab my assault rifle, put my earpiece in, and leave out the back door to go get in position down the street at the city library. Luckily, it's starting to get dark, so I check my surroundings before climbing up the back of the library.

"This is Uncle Jack. Is everyone in place and ready to rock?"

"This is Soli, and I'm in place."

"This is Dev. I'm all set."

"Alright, you two, let's execute this as clean as possible. We need to make sure he is alive because we need him for questioning. His detail needs to be dead on impact or close to it. Remember, major arteries, the center chest, or headshot. We've been tracking this fucker for long enough and it's time we get what we need from him. Then we can take him out."

"10-4 boss," Dev responds.

Since this Saber-Forsst Mod rifle was higher powered than my other, I set up my tripod and adjusted my sights to see inside the meeting room. I watched him as he shook hands and is kissing ass of the higher-ranking officials.

"Target is on the move and headed towards the door. His detail consists of four men. Two in the front and two in the back."

As he walked out of the door, I got my sights in position to hit him. Out of nowhere, shots were fired and Kupp was down.

"WHO TOOK THE SHOT?!" Unc is screaming over the earpiece.

"Looking for the perp now, Unc! Looks like the shot came from inside of the building!", Shunny radios in.

"Shit! We didn't account for that. Police are going to be everywhere soon. We need to skate. Leave the area immediately", Unc was frantic.

I break down my weapon and pack my shit up. I slid down the grappling hook rope and ran for my bike. I pushed it down the back alley and started it once I got far enough from the library. As I circle the block to drop my gun in the back of Unc's pickup, I see Dre. He was walking at a fast pace down the block from behind the building where Kupp was meeting, and he was wearing all black tactical gear.

He had a bag like mine. The size bag that could carry an assault rifle. What the hell was he doing here and at the same time as us? And why the hell could he have wanted Kupp dead? This had to be some CIA shit. I sped past him and kept going until I reached our meet-up point to regroup.

"WHAT THE FUCK WAS THAT?!" Devin is heated.

"I think the CIA is involved. I saw one of their agents leaving the scene in a hurry."

"You know who it is?" Unc turned to me confused.

"Yea, it's Dre McCargo."

"McCargo?" Devin is silent and walks to the window.

"It's something deeper than we know if the CIA is killing an FBI agent. I need to make a call. You two sit tight."

Unc got up and went to the back to make a call to The League's higher-ups. Either someone knows who we're going after and why, or they have their own motives to keep him quiet. I turn the news on and see a report about the shooting.

Kupp was in ICU but wasn't dead. He had been shot in the shoulder and back. Looks like Dre wasn't a good shooter if it was him. Knowing the FBI and the CIA, they were going to try and touch him before anyone else. It was time to tap an OG in. I call Grandma J.

"Grandma J, we need you."

"I'll be there, baby."

One thing about Grandma J is that she's always up for a challenge. She got dressed as a nurse and walked in there just as easy. We already had hospital badge access from previous assignments, so she was undetected. Shunny sent her all his stats and his room number. While Grandma J is upstairs, she is going to hand a fake hospital transfer to the doctor and nurse staff so we can get Kupp out. We call Robin to bring an ambulance and some paramedic uniforms.

"Hello, my name is Jean and I have been sent here on behalf of Mr. Kupp's family. They would like to have him transferred to a facility closer to home for his safety and I see based on his charts he is currently stable."

"Well hello Jean, I am Doctor Monk. I don't recall seeing the transfer papers in the system. And yes, the patient is stable."

"Doctor Monk, would you mind checking again? I have the discharge and the transfer request right here. Please take a look."

"Wait one moment. Let me check my system." The doctor took Grandma J's bait and Shunny had planted the transfer papers in the system just in time.

"Alright, Nurse Jean, I see the transfer order and I will work on getting Mr. Kupp transferred immediately. Thank you for your patience." Grandma J smiles and calls down to us.

"We're all good to go, kids. Kupp will be downstairs shortly. Is the transportation ready?"

"We're set, Grandma J. Robin just got here a few minutes ago and we're changed."

Hell, with so much drama going on I had forgotten all about Anderson being at my house. He just so happened to text me in the midst of it.

Anderson: Hey sweet cheeks, it's getting kind of late. Are you alright? I haven't heard from you since your note. How about we do a late dinner and a walk around the city? Talk to you soon!

Aww man he is so sweet. I hate that we had to meet this lifetime. Maybe it would've worked. He deserves so much. I start to text him back when Grandma J and some hospital staff start rolling Kupp out the front doors and loading him into the back of the ambulance. We pull off and head to Grandma J's safe house.

"Good Job, everyone! Grandma J is proud of you. Now I got it from here."

"Mama, I'm staying here with you."

"Come on in son, let me show you a thing or two about torture. I got a new truth serum too. Maybe we can try it out on this fella."

Grandma J, Unc, and Dev go inside, and I head out to go get my car. When I pull up to my house. Whyyyyy is my sister here already? I walk inside to see her eating.

"Umm Oshun, boo boo. How are you eating before the owner of the house?"

"Sis when you said Anderson was in town, I knowwww you did not think that we weren't coming over here to eat."

"We? Who is we?"

146

"Oh, Pops is in the bathroom. Anderson made vegan food and Pops ate it. Haha Anderson you might replace Rashad!"

"SHUNNY! Shut up" I smile at Anderson nervously.

"Rashad? That must be your ex huh?" He smiles at me.

"Yea something like that. I'm going to shower. I'll be right back," I turn to go upstairs.

"Sweet cheeks, why are you dressed like a paramedic?" Oh shit, I forgot to change.

"She volunteers sometimes. Anderson this is delicious. I hope you serve some of this at our new restaurant."

"Oh, that's cool. You didn't tell me that," he shrugs and keeps cooking.

"Haha, yes I do a lot to serve our community," There was Pops, my savior. He didn't know exactly what was going on, but he always has my back. I smile at him and walk upstairs to shower. As I wash off, I am dreading this conversation I have to have with Anderson.

I don't know how he's going to react. I mean technically we're not a couple, we're just dating. I hate this type of conflict. I hated it when I had to divorce Shad. I hop out of the shower and get dressed so I can eat dinner before those two eat it all.

After dinner, my additional guests clear out. I help Anderson clean the kitchen and we both pour a glass of wine. Normalcy felt good for the moment I had it. Having a team made life easier than it was when I was doing solo missions. Shad caught the brunt of that stress. Anderson caught me in my head as we sat by the fireplace.

"A penny for your thoughts."

"Oh, I'm sorry. I'm just tired." He began to massage my shoulders.

"What can I do to help? I know your sister kind of put you on blast a little huh? Exes are a difficult topic."

"Yea, going into it you never really expect your marriage to end."

"I didn't expect mine to end either, but we were young. Trying to build my business, I wasn't always there. She miscarried while I was gone on a business trip, and we never recovered from it. We blamed one another. We became distant. The arguments became more frequent. I would take it all back if I could. I would take her back if I could."

"Wow, I'm so sorry to hear that. I didn't know you were married. Marriage is hard work. I wish I could've done things differently too. Communicated and listened more, you know?"

"Listen Solice, I'm not here to replace anyone. I'm just here to share space and time with you as long as you allow me the opportunity to. If that comes to an end, I'll be happy for the time we spent. I turn 40 years old on December 25. That's two months from now. I am learning to take things a day at a time. Even a moment at a time. Sweet cheeks, you're only 32. You have plenty of time to figure it out. If you want your marriage back, fight for it. No questions asked."

I'm surprised at how chill he is about me fighting to get Shad back. It was almost like a weight lifted off my shoulders.

"I really, I mean really, like you Anderson, but I love my ex-husband. I don't want to hurt you."

"Ms. Solice, you will not hurt me, and we will always be friends. You saved my life. I am indebted to you. Now I will ask you to enjoy the rest of our weekend together."

"I can do that."

He leans down to kiss my lips and we keep kissing. We kiss like it was goodbye and ultimately it probably will be. We make love again, but this time it is slower, longer, and intentional. I stare at him and rub his face as he sleeps. He held me tight. He was right. I had to live in the moment because tomorrow he would be leaving.

When we wake up in the morning, we just stare into each other's eyes for a moment. He scoops me up out of bed and carries me to the tub. He runs us some bath water then slides in and motions for me to join him. I take his hand to get in then I lay back against him. He kisses my ear and neck. Woo, he is making sure I don't forget him. I kiss his hand.

"You're a special woman, Solice. Never forget that. You'll always have a place in my heart."

"You're a very special man. I just wish we had more time to live in this moment."

"Don't worry about the time. Always enjoy the now." We finish our bath, and he goes downstairs to make our breakfast. We sat for breakfast and continue to talk.

Once we were done, I took him to the airport, and we kiss for the last time. I hope he and his ex-wife can figure things out. It seems like he still loves her while holding space for me. I know for myself that people grow and change. If Rashad wasn't who he is, I probably would continue things with Anderson. He doesn't deserve to be mixed up in my mess of a life though.

Him getting shot was enough for me to want to distance myself from him. It also made me wonder how I would keep Shad safe. Anderson gets out of the car and grabs his bags. He smiles and blows me a kiss then walks into the airport. Damn. I hope I know what I'm doing letting him go.

I drive off and start to think about how things were going to go with Shad telling Kayla it was over. I kind of feel bad for her. I don't think Shad used her as a placeholder and I think he genuinely cared about her, but he just loves me. For her sake, I hope she isn't as crazy as she looks because I'll have to kick her ass.

OLD FRIENDS

I got my baby back, baby back, Rashad's baby back ribs!
YEAAAA. Shit, I honestly did not think this day would
happen. Ever since I saw Solice at the coffee house, I felt
so guilty. Like I was cheating on my wife guilty. To see
the look on her face and the way she walked out of the
door. I couldn't bear to see her like that again.

Plus, Kayla had been acting mad weird. She would
be clingy one day and distant another. She turned it up a
notch after she finally met Solice in person. Once she
found out that me and Solice were back friends, her vibe
changed.

And Soli, my god, something was different about
her today. Maybe she is feeling this Anderson cat and he's
making her happy. I want Solice to be happy, no matter
who she chooses. If she comes back tomorrow and tells
me she can't be with me, I'll have to be ok with that. First
and foremost, I still gotta let Kayla go. That possessive
and clingy stuff has never been my M.O. She also knows
exactly who she was and what she looked like. I still have
pictures of us around my house.

"Hello Kayla, can we talk?"

"Hey Sexy! Do you want me to come by?"

"Nah meet me at my Mom's office around 4:30 pm."

"Alright, I'll see you then."

Solice had just left so I knew I had to figure out what I was going to tell Kayla. We had only been dating for 18 months but I knew my heart wasn't there, no matter how hard I tried. I wasn't in the business of wasting people's time or breaking hearts, so I had to be honest. I keep painting until she walks through the door.

"Rashad! I'm here. It looks nice in here, Boo!"

"Ah, Thanks, Kay. So, I need to talk to you about something."

"What is it? Are you asking? Yes, Rashad! Yes, I will...," she starts freaking out and hyperventilating and shit.

"Whoa whoa, no, no it's not that."

"You want to move in together?"

"It's not that either." She started to look confused at this point and I knew I had to spit it out.

"Kay, my heart just isn't into our relationship, and I don't think that's fair to you. You deserve to be with someone who is all in."

"It's her isn't it," she peers at me. I thought her head was about to start spinning.

"I just have some things I need to figure out for myself. This is hard for me and I'm sure it's hard for you as well. Yes, she is a part of it."

"Fuck you, Rashad. I knew by the way you've been acting since you and her became 'friends' again and then how you've been acting since we saw her at the coffee shop, that you still loved her." She slaps me and storms out of the office. That slap was a relief. I hadn't broken up with a woman in years.

Buzz Buzz Buzz.

Man, who is this calling me now?

"Yo?"

"What up, boy?"

"What up, Moe"

"Ain't nothing. Over here painting mom duke's office."

"I need to holla at you about something."

"What is it, Dre? Man, you've been ghost for months. What the hell is going on with you?"

"I'll stop by your place later. Hit me when you leave out."

"Ight bet."

That nigga is acting mad weird. Oh well. I've got shit to do. I'll deal with him later. Mina is at my parents' house so I can fly out in the morning. I have to go to Texas for a couple of weeks for a project. It should be fun to network with some other architects and learn some new stuff. I clean up all my painting supplies and head to the front to lock up the office. When I walk out the door, I see that I have a flat and I figure that's no coincidence considering the convo I just had with Kayla. I log into my insurance app and order roadside assistance. Damn, I guess I brought this shit on myself, huh?

But back to Dre. What in the hell was so important that he couldn't tell me over the phone? Me and Dre met back in high school when we played against one another in football and track. He was always hella competitive but a good dude from what I could tell. We crossed paths again when I transferred to Bowie State.

We balled on the same team this time and he put me on to being an RA. From there we stayed cool, hell he was even one of my witnesses when me and Solice got married. Dre always kept it a buck with me, so whatever he was about to tell me had to be something serious. Especially since he wouldn't tell me over the phone. Knowing that he works for the alphabet boys.

Ever since he's been in the CIA, he has been a little different. I remember when he first went in, he got sick mysteriously. He lost all bodily functions like he was a vegetable. Then all of a sudden, he was good again, traveling the world and shit. I never asked him about it. I was just there for my boy.

Guess I should order some Chinese while I wait. Maybe they'll get here at the same time as the roadside. My phone starts going crazy and I look down and it's Kayla. Lord, I've been trying to be a good man. I send her to ignore then check my cameras around the house to make sure her crazy ass isn't over there poking around. I change my passcodes on everything just to cover my ass.

Roadside pulls up with my new tire and so does my food. This must be the second win of the day for me. I send Dre a text letting him know I'll be heading home in about 30 minutes. I sit on the steps and eat my food. It was starting to get dark, so I got up and drove home. Dre didn't respond until two hours later. One thing Solice always taught me was to keep my shit near me. It didn't matter who it was.

Ding Dong!

"Hey, Bro, I'm at the gate."
"Ight man, I'll open it for you."
I slid my .22 under my coffee table and hid a blade in the sofa. Then I got up to open the door.
"Come on in man, have a seat."
"You'll need to have one too after this." He had a book bag and was dressed in all black.
"Alright, what's up bro? You seem a little shaken."
He started to go into his book bag and all I could do was watch him and look at the gun under the table. He pulls a huge file out of his bag.
"Look at this file and tell me who you see."
"A file? What kind of file would you need to show me?"
I grab the file and open it up. I start to look through it and notice the silhouette of the woman resembled my baby. The locations where she has traveled to handle the wine business. The posture and the stance she has when she shoots. I had seen her shoot all types of guns over the years, and she always had the same posture and focus. I never questioned it because of who her family is. As I

keep looking through the files, it listed her as a Jane Doe Assassin.

"Dre, what the fuck is this? Jane Doe Assassin?"

"I was hoping you could give me some answers." I keep looking at the pictures and I get a side profile of her face.

"I-I-I-IS this Solice?!"

"It seems to be as such, brother. I have been tracking these high-profile hits for a while and everywhere I track, she seems to be." He knew by the look on my face I had no clue. Man, I am sick to my stomach. I start scratching my head.

"Are you sure this is her? How can it be her? Is she living a double life? I don't understand this here. I'm a smart man, but this shit here, Dre? Nah. Nah, man. That cannot be my baby, man," I'm shaking my head and putting the files back on the table.

"Think about it, Rashad. Look at the patterns in your marriage. The absence. The secrecy. Look at her family. All of them are trained to go. That's sis, so I brought this to you before my job. I'm out here playing dumb at work. Rashad, I saw her tonight on her Mom's old bike."

"Her Mom's bike? I haven't seen that bike since Ma Ang died. I thought she got rid of that shit."

"I shouldn't even be telling you this, but we had the same target. I peeped her climbing down from a library. I'm sure she saw me, too."

"WHAT? She was in the middle of a h-h-h-it?"

"She's pretty damn good too, especially with the knowledge you've given her about architecture. She knows where and how to hide."

"How did you see her then?"

"She's good, but I'm better", he looks down at his phone and it was his boss calling. The target was transferred, and they were now unable to locate him.

"Look man, I gotta go. Keep this file and don't let anyone see it. You stay safe."

"Hey man! How do I protect her or get her out?"

"You can't. Just learn how to protect yourself. Love you, man", and just like that he was out.

I must've stayed up looking through that file for hours. Shit, how naïve had I been? I get the love of my life back and could lose her all over again. I gotta protect my wife by any means necessary. I'll call Pops tomorrow after I land in Houston. I tried to get some rest, but I kept having dreams about Soli getting shot. I keep waking up in a cold sweat.

When I wake up again, it was time for me to head out. I got myself together and head out of the door. I try to call Dre from the truck but it's going straight to voicemail. I call Soli and that went to voicemail too. I hope they're not out here trying to kill each other. Damn.

I walk into the airport and shoot Soli a text. Nothing. Now I am getting more paranoid. I finish going through TSA and start walking to my terminal. I guess I'm just going to have to trust she is fine. I turn my music on and take a seat. My watch vibrates and I see it's her texting me back.

Lice: Hey Sexy, you're looking good

I look around because how in the hell can she see what I look like? This is some spy crap. I text back 'How would you know?' Then I look around again. She goes black and doesn't respond. The flight attendant begins to announce the sections boarding the plane. I stand up and look to grab my bag and it's gone. What the hell? I start looking around and I see some random small man holding it while boarding for first class.

"EXCUSE ME!" I run towards him and grab his shoulder.

"Aye man where in the hell do yo…" She turns around and smiles.

"Man Lice, I was about to whoop your ass!"

"Haha! Got you!" I pick her and the bag up and throw them over my shoulder then walk in the tunnel.

"Sir! Sir! You can't keep her on your shoulder. It is a safety hazard."

I wave off the flight attendant and put Soli down.

"Girl, what in the hell are you doing on this flight?"

"I have some work to do in Texas. Pops was contacted by this lady in Houston about us being their primary vendor. And I sure didn't lie. You look good in this chocolate suit!"

"Uh-huh. Thank you. You could've told me. You know I had to be in Houston all week for this conference."

"That would've taken the fun out of everything. Plus, I have a long trip coming up next week and I decided that I am going to hang out with you this week." She nudges me.

"One question though. Why are you walking around here looking like a little boy? I mean damn, Lice."

"I like to keep a low profile when I fly. I'm comfy in a jogging suit and some jays." I shake my head and walk onto the plane.

"Where are you sitting?"

"You know I like window seats. I'm over here."

"Yo, you're mad crafty. How did you end up with the seat beside me?"

"I have my ways. Now sit."

She plops down in the seat. She seems to be super giddy. I haven't seen her like this in a while. I smile at her and sit down beside her. She lays her head on my shoulder and steals my other headphone like normal. I kiss her forehead and close my eyes. I felt at peace knowing that she was in my sight.

When I wake up, it's almost time to land and she is still knocked out. I start reading over my presentations. As I was reading, she started mumbling in her sleep. I look over at her and she is flinching. It looks like she is having a nightmare.

"Baby, wake up. Soli wake up baby"
She jumps up gasping for air. *What the hell?*

"Soli?"

"Yes, baby! I'm sorry I was having a bad dream."

"What was it about?"

"I don't even know. It was a lot going on and I was falling."

I rub her shoulders and kiss her forehead. We start descending into Houston. I notice her staring out the window. I wonder if she was telling the truth about her dream. By the time we land, I grab our bags and we head off the plane.

I got a message that my hotel was canceled while we were in the air.

"Ah man, what the hell?"

"What's wrong baby?"

"They canceled my hotel room."

"Oh no, let me see if I can find somewhere."

I knew she had something to do with it but I'm going to let her have her fun. We walk to the departure area and find my driver. He leads us to the SUV and puts our bags in the back.

"Take us to the Galleria Houston, please."

I look over at her and smirk as I rub her hand. She always has something up her sleeve, but I could tell she was making the effort for us to spend time together. I appreciate that. We pull up to the Galleria and it is gigantic. Hell, it was better than the hotel I had picked anyway. She does have excellent taste. We get out of the SUV and grab our bags to head inside. I wonder if she's got a hit down here. She's never been on a business trip with me before. I don't see any other bags. Does she travel with her weapons?

We check into the hotel, and she is all smiles. I kiss her lips and we go into the elevator. She stares up at me with an evil little smirk on her face. She would have to wait until later to take advantage of me because I have a seminar to go to, and I'm on the panel. We get to the penthouse floor, and I look over at her. This is what she smiled about.

We walk into our room, and it looks like it is a scene out of a movie. Room service had already delivered our brunch. We sit and eat before it was time for me to head out. I shower and get dressed. She stretches out on the bed and falls asleep. I kiss her forehead and leave out. I hope she behaves herself while I'm gone.

I walk down to the convention center and get ready for the seminar. Once everyone was seated, I began the seminar. After about an hour, everyone's phones started going off with alerts. What the hell was going on? A senator had been shot to death down the street from us. Security came in to evacuate everyone and sent us back to our rooms.

I ran down the street back to our hotel. I open the door and there she is. In the same spot that I left her. There's no way she could've done this right? Or at least that's what I want to believe. I stood there for a minute to see if she would move and notice that I was back.
She didn't move so I went to her side and shook her. She slowly opens her eyes and looks at me.

"Hey, Sleepyhead."

"Hey Handsome, what's up?"

"You look well rested. You've been doing a lot of sleeping."

"I'm just tired from all the traveling I've been doing." *And killing*, I thought to myself.

"Well, how was your conference?"

"Funny you ask, it was interrupted by an assassination."

"An assassination? Who, Where, and when? Are you okay?"

She seems genuinely concerned.

"A senator was shot in the head down the street. I'm surprised that you didn't hear your phone go off with alerts."

"Hmm, it looks like it has been on airplane mode since we boarded the airplane. What senator was it?"

"Kyle Tate."

"Oh man, I've heard bad things about that guy. He probably had a few enemies. Any info on the shooter?"

"Not that I've heard. They rushed us out of there so fast, we barely got any details."

"Wow, that's crazy."

She smiles and shrugs then turns the TV on. She only has one bag and I doubt she snuck an assault rifle on the plane, and she wasn't arrested. I'm caught in thought when she comes over to me, pushes me down on the bed, and makes me forget about the shooting and the conference.

I kiss her on her forehead then go to shower as she falls back asleep. When I get out the shower, I check my phone. I have a message from Dre, telling me to be safe. Hmm. Maybe he knows something I don't. I still have some suspicions but for now, I'm going to enjoy this time with my baby.

When I wake up in the morning she is gone. Where the hell is the woman? I look over and see breakfast sitting on the table with a note that she is going for a run. I don't know if I should believe it or not. Oh well, there's nothing I can really do about it at this moment. I might as well go ahead and eat.

***

On the other side of town…

"Shunny, I think I'm going to go for a two-for-one today."

"What are you talking about sis?"

"Guess who's in Houston?"

"Shoot, well that's all you do."

"Haha, jokey jokes today huh? Marty Peoples!"

"Marty Peoples. Marty Peoples?"

"You know Marty, the guy that owns the chemical company that polluted all that water in a few black communities and never did anything to fix it."

"Ohhhh, him. Do your thing girl! He's low priority, but still on the list."

"Say no more."

Click.

I know I have to make this quick because Shad was probably awake already. I pull my mask over my face and tuck my pistol in my combat belt under my shirt. He's walking into the parking garage, and I follow.

I duck down behind a SUV not too far from him. He hasn't started his car yet, so I roll under the cars until I get under his.

I put a tracker and a disabling device on it. I slide from under the car near the back and wait for him to get out. He tries to turn it on, but it stalls.

"What the fuck is going on with this thing!", he yells as he gets out and slams the door.

"Put your hands behind your back and quietly get into the car," I put my gun to the back of his head, and he slowly unlocks the doors and gets back in.

"Who the hell are you?"

"Now, now, is that any way to speak to a lady?"

"My apologies, ma'am. What is this pertaining to? I do not carry cash on me."

"Oh, I don't want your money. I want you to fix the water systems in the communities you fucked up and pay the medical bills of those suffering because of it," I tap the gun against the side of his temple.

"I-I-I can't do that."

"Hmm, I see. Well maybe I will keep visiting you until it is done. Matter a fact. Let me incentivize you." I call Tobin.

"Hit the button."

"That was just confirmation of an explosion in one of your facilities and after a while your business will be in shambles, so I suggest you find a way to make it right before I find you again."

His phone started ringing off the hook and I got out of the car then ran down the stairwell. I pick up my bag out of the trash can and I leave my mask on until I find bathroom in a grocery store. I run in the stall and change then walk out of the store. Well, that was a fun way to start the day. Guess I should be getting back to my man.

IT'S ON

As soon as I found out about what Solice was into, I knew I had to go to one of the men that had been protecting her, Pops. He always kept it real with me. He could tell that whatever it was, it's bothering me to the point that I had to come to see him in person. I had talked to him while I was on my work trip, but all I could think about was how I was going to go about this. By the time I landed back in D.C., I was a nervous wreck. Wondering if Pops would even know what was going on. I had a thousand questions. Maybe I should've asked Grandma J first. Maybe Uncle Jack.

I leave the airport and head to Pop's crib. I pull into the driveway and take a deep breath. I wonder has he known about Solice and how Ma Ang would handle this situation with Soli. I get out of the car and walk to the front door then ring the doorbell.

"It's open, son! Come on in."

"Hey Pops! What's up?"

"Oh, nothing just in here cleaning up. Have a seat. What can I do for you today?"

"Pops I gotta ask you, something man."

"Shoot."

"Umm, I don't even know where to start for real."

"I assume since you don't know where to start that it is about my hardheaded daughter."

"Yes sir, I just found out some crazy stuff from Dre."

"Like what? Is she in danger? Because he works for the CIA, right?"

"He does and he gave me this file" I hand Pops the file on Soli. He didn't seem the least bit upset as he read.

"Well, damn son. It's about time you have the same conversation with Soli that I had with her mother." I was confused.

"What conversation was that Pops?"

"Well, there's no easy way to tell you about the inner workings of our family. When I met your mother-in-law, she was just a Marine or so I thought. We took a trip to Lagos and all hell broke loose. We were in the middle of one of her missions and she was mad.

And when I say missions, I'm not talking about the Marines. I was scared to death, but I knew I wouldn't let a damn thing happen to the woman I loved. When I saw how she fought and shot her way out of that situation, that was it for me. She had to start talking and telling me

167

what the hell was going on. That little woman we all love so much was not only a Marine, but she was also a trained assassin for an unknown organization.

Your wife is a trained assassin for the same organization. Mama J is a trained assassin. Long story even shorter. Everyone in this family is trained to go in some sort of fashion. That's how we were raised and that's how my daughters were raised. Now initially, this was not my conversation to have with you. This was supposed to be Solice's cross to bear but since you asked me, I'm going to tell you because you love my daughter. You are a part of this family.

If I doubted for any minute that you did not love my daughter and my family, I wouldn't tell you shit. Rashad, I've known you for a very long time. Now with all this new information, you tell me what you need me to do. You are always going to be her husband whether y'all are separated or not. I know you want to protect her but fight beside her not against her or in front of her. And TALK! That's how y'all are going to make it this time around. Whether you want to wait for her to tell you or let her know that you know."

I am speechless. It was too much to process, but as a man, I had to protect the woman I loved. That was by any means necessary, all day, every day. If I wanted her back, that meant I had to take all of her, not just the parts I love about her.

"Pops, I need you to teach me how to protect her. The same way you protected Ma Angie. I can't let her feel like I'm not in this with her. I imagine that's the reason why she filed for divorce in the first place. I wish she would've told me from the jump. I haven't been able to sleep since finding out. I'm fighting the want to ask her where she is and what she is doing because I don't want her to lie to me."

"Say no more, son. I'll call up Jack and we'll get you squared away. This will not be an easy road. It took us years to train Solice and Oshun. We're going to work you hard. She loves you and will protect you to no limit and she thought that divorcing you would distance you from this but when it's real, no distance in this world will keep you all from each other. You two are magnets. Don't let her you know yet."

"I'll do whatever it takes."
Pops and I dapped each other up and continued to talk.

For weeks I trained with Pops and Uncle Jack. These two old heads wore me out. I thought I was in shape. Occasionally, I would let Soli wear me out with her neighborhood runs just so I could be closer to her. The mental part of it was the wildest. But I knew as long as I kept my mind on protecting Soli I would be good.

I can only imagine how they held it down mentally because it was kicking my ass. Uncle Jack had me at the range shooting every gun in sight and even tampering with explosives. I can't lie I was scared to mess with Grandma J because I wasn't with getting poisoned. Every time Soli would leave town it would tear me up inside thinking of her getting hurt or even merking someone. This is the life she had been trying to shield me from. Well, at least she thought she was still shielding me from it.

Ring. Ring. Ring.

"Yo, this is Shad."

"Hey baby boy!"

"Hey mom, what's up?"

"Nothing, just checking on my baby. How are you doing? I haven't seen you in a while. You want to do lunch?"

"Yea I know mom, I've been hella busy. Sure, when would you like to do lunch?"

"Maybe in about an hour. Is Solice around?"

"Nah she's out of town. Why?"

"I thought maybe she's been taking so much of your time that you forgot about me."

"Oh mom, it's nothing like that. I've just been working, and she's been out of town a lot lately."

"You two need to slow down and make time for each other. Remember time and communication. Open and honest communication has been an issue for you both in the past. If you are working on a future, you have to make that a priority."

"We will, Ma. Where do you want me to meet you?"

"Meet me at the Oyster House on 3rd."

"Alright, I'll see you in an hour."

I hop in the shower so I can get ready to meet Moms. When I get out of the shower, I see I have 3 missed calls from an unknown number but no voicemail. Hmm. That's weird. Somebody must be playing on my damn phone. I hope Soli is good. I haven't heard from her in a few hours. I get dressed and take Mina out for a walk then Facetime her.

"Hello!"

"Yo baby yo?!"

"Oh, hey Pooh!"

"What are you doing? Why are you sweating like that?" She probably just got done popping a nigga. Shit, I don't need to think like that.

"I just got back from a run. See? Let me see my baby, Rashad!" She angled the phone down to show off her body suit and sneakers.

"Here Mina, your mammy is on the phone."

"Haha, not mammy. Hey Mina Bina! Mommy misses you! I will be home tomorrow!"

"Oh? When were you going to tell Daddy you were coming home?

"When I got back in my room, Husband. How was your day? What have you been up to?"

"Nothing much, getting some work done. I stopped by to check on Pops. Getting ready to go have lunch with Mom Dukes."

"Tell her I said hello. You two enjoy, baby. Call me later. I'm going to hop in the shower. I love you so much Pooh, and I can't wait to see you tomorrow!"

"I love you, Honey Bun."

Damn, so it wasn't her calling me. Who the hell has been blowing up my phone? Probably Kayla's crazy ass.

I take Mina back in the house then lock up to head out. As I'm riding down the interstate, I keep noticing this car behind me every time I look in my rearview. Man, I know ain't nobody following me. I switch lanes and they switch lanes. Shit. I need to get off the interstate. Is my gun still in here? I start opening my glove box. It ain't in there. Damn. I check the middle console. It ain't there either.

Oh hell, I'm screwed. Wait. I reach behind the passenger seat and here it is in the seat pocket. I pull it out and sit it on my lap. I pull off the interstate and find an alley to cut through then stop. I look in the rear review and they speed past the alley. I finally let out a deep breath and called Mom to let her know I'm running late. I put my truck in reverse and backed out of the alley. Too bad I didn't get the license plate.

I speed off and hop back on a ramp. I know I couldn't tell Soli what happened because she would try to burn D.C. down to find out who was following me. I know I couldn't tell Mom because she would shit a brick and try to lock me away.

I had to call Pops and let him know once I got done with my Mom. I parked in front of the restaurant, put the gun in my waistband, then walked inside. I knew this wouldn't be the end of some weird shit happening. I had to keep this to myself until I could figure out how to address Solice's 'other' job.

I finally arrive at Oyster House and go inside to sit down with Mom. She was waiting patiently while reading her book by the window.

"Hey, Mom!"

"About time, Rashad! I thought you were going to leave me here to starve."

172

"Ah come on, Mom. I got caught in some traffic."

"Uh-huh, come on, sit down. I ordered some appetizers. What have you been eating? You're looking kind of bulky, son."

"I've just been working out a little more. That's all. Trying to stay healthy for when I have a kid, you know?"

"SOLICE IS PREGNANT ALREADY?"

"Maaaa, chill. No, she isn't pregnant. Just preparing for the future, you know?"

"Uh-huh. I haven't seen you look like this since you were in college. You look happy though. I'm glad to see that shimmer in your eyes again. I never liked that Kaysha. Solice will always be my daughter-in-law. If y'all are serious, I will support it."

"Kayla, Mom. Yea she wasn't for me. I do feel bad about the way I ended things but I'm glad I did it when I did. I couldn't fight my feelings for Solice anymore. I was struggling between exploring a new relationship and missing what I lost. I want to be a good man, but I also don't want to continue to lead someone on. Me and Solice had been talking and hanging out for the last few months. She confirmed everything that I needed to know in that time."

"What did she confirm?"

"That we never lost anything. We still enjoyed each other's company. We still love to laugh together. We still feel butterflies when we see each other."

"True love never dies, son. Not everyone will get to experience it. But, when you do, hold on to it. Protect it. Nurture it. Give it everything."

I smile at my Mom and nod. We order our entrees and keep chopping it up. One thing about Mom Dukes, she always listens and gives the best advice. That's my heart. Now it was time to wait for the other piece of my heart to get back home.

LOVE

Soli had gotten home early this morning after taking a red-eye home from New York. As we lay in bed, I started thinking about how important Solice is to me. We had been back together a few months and it felt like it did when we first got married. Hell, she even gave me butterflies every once in a while. We started couples therapy as soon as we got back together because I wanted to show her how serious I was about us being back together.

I still think about the file Dre gave me. I locked the folder away so she wouldn't find it when she came over. Unfortunately, I hadn't told her about the shit Kayla had been up to either. That was for Kayla's protection though because if Lice found out about the unknown calls, random flat tires, and popping up where I am, she would kill her. Like literally kill her. I am still wrapping my head around my baby being an assassin. It's mad wild to think I would ever say that.

"Do you want to go up to Niagara Falls this weekend?" I ask as I rub her leg. Niagara Falls was one of our places of peace. It brought back so many memories of when times were a little simpler.

"Hell yea! Let's go! You know I'm never going to say no to a trip to our favorite place." She smiles so beautifully with excitement.

"Don't pack anything, let's just take ourselves and go."

"Okay!"

She raises her eyebrows and pokes her lips out. At this point, I knew she had no idea that I was planning to propose again. All her closest friends and family were already there waiting for us. I had the hotel and the rooftop restaurant picked out. I had her old ring upgraded. She loved gemstones way more than diamonds, so I made sure me and her sister picked out a beautiful pear morganite gemstone and rose gold ring.

She was always in black, so I wanted to make sure she added some color to her wardrobe.
"Hey Babe, look in the closet I got you something." As she looked in the closet, she looked back at me with a grin. Before her Mom died she always wore bright vibrant colors so I thought why not add some more color back to her life?

"RASHADDDDD! When did you do all of this? It looks like a freaking rainbow in here. And you KNOW I love yellow." She pulled out the yellow sundress and held it up against her bare body.

"Put it on, baby." I loved the way that she admired herself in the mirror and her smile.

"I am! Let me slide this sexy thang on down."

I laughed as she slid it on, being the goof that she is. She looked damn good, especially with that thigh peeking out at me like she was Ms. Trinidad.

"IIIIII wanna be your man....", I sang as she sashayed around the room. It amazed me that after all this time we never lost our connection. I've always loved her.

"What else do I need?"

"Your passport and let me take care of everything else."

"Say less! I'm ready, but if you keep standing there naked, I'll have to take advantage of you, Mr. King."

"There will be plenty of time for you to take advantage of me when we get to Canada, we've got a plane waiting on us."

"A plane? Look at you bougie…"

"Only the best for my baby."

"I know that's right," she said as she bit her lip and grabbed my dick. Lord, I hope we make it out of the house. I got dressed and grabbed my wallet then took Mina outside for her morning walk. Once me and Mina were done walking, I put all our bags in the truck and let Mina hop in the backseat.

There she was, beaming as she skipped down the steps in yellow Jordan 1 Retros. All I could do is shake my head and laugh because this was her in all her glory.

"Had to break out the matching Jays huh?"

"You know it!"

"Haha, my baby."

We both hop in and head to the airport. It was good to see her so happy again. She seemed so distracted most times I don't even think she noticed that she hadn't smiled in a while. She definitely didn't notice all the time I had been spending with Pops and Uncle Jack.

When we arrive at the airport, she hops out like a kid in a candy store.

"THIS IS THE JET WE'RE TAKING?"

"Yes, love this is the jet."

"THE PILOT AND CREW ARE BLACK, TOO?"

"Yes, Solice. The pilot and crew are black, too."

"That boy is good! Good, I tell you! A round of applause for my ex-husband, boyfriend, future husband, and baby's daddy!"

"Baby daddy huh? Solice, get on the plane."

"Yes, Daddddyyyyy!"

I grabbed the bags out of the back and whistled for Mina to come on behind me. We are finally heading back to the place where it all began. I don't think I have been up here in years.

She looked out the window happily while rubbing Mina's head. As I watched her stare out the window, I thought about all the shit Dre had told me about some hits that may be connected to Soli. I thought about that file he gave me. I couldn't figure out why and how, but I knew I needed to. I wonder if this has anything to do with Ma Ang's disappearance. This woman means the world to me, and I'd do anything in this world to protect her, I just know I can't do that with us apart.

"Baby, look!" I look over at her as she smiles while looking out the window.

"What is it, love?"

"We're flying over the falls."

"Baby this is only the beginning," I smirk and sat back in my seat.

After flying over the waterfalls, we landed at the airport and got off the plane. I had a driver waiting to take us to the Seneca Niagara Resort and Casino. Once at the hotel, we went to go get a couple's massage, while the hotel prepared for our surprise evening wedding. While her head was down, I motioned for the masseuse to bring the ring box out of my pants pocket. I got up from the table and got on one knee in front of her headrest.

"All done ma'am, take your time getting up from the table," the masseuse said as she walked out of the room.

"Wooo baby that was a breath of fresh air," Solice said as she lifted her head from the headrest, locking eyes with me.

"Rashad, what the hell are you doing down there?" Her eyes got big as saucers.

"What do you say Slim, you wanna do it again?", I asked her as I held up the ring.

"Awww baby! I will do it again any and every time after that!"

Soli jumps up from the table and falls into my arms. We embrace and kiss with so much love. I kiss her on her forehead, and we go to our suite. I couldn't even get into the room before she began to rip off my robe and we made love like it was the first night we met. After we were done, I let her sleep so I could hop in the shower and get dressed. I wrote her a note that said,

"To my again, Beautiful Future Wife, I love you. Since the day our separation began, I never forgave myself for not fighting hard enough for you. I regret the time we let pass without us being together and no matter what, I am always going to have your back. You are my past, my current, and my future. That will never change. I have wanted to be YOUR husband since the day you opened your goofy lips to speak to me. Baby, you move me.
Baby, you're my muse. Baby, you're my heart in human form and I want you to know that. Meet me at 8 pm at the rooftop elevator. Leave the guns…

Love Always,

Shad

P.S. you're going to get pregnant hopping on me like that…BAYBEEE OOOH WEEE and you let me let loose? Shittttt"

    I lay the letter on the nightstand on her side and place a sunflower next to it. I go upstairs to the rooftop to check on the setup and our families to make sure everything is good. If I know my baby, she's still going to bring a gun with her in unfamiliar places. They say know your devil and this time around, that little demon is not getting away.

I call her cell phone to make sure she is awake. My nerves were shot to hell. "Solice are you...."

"Rashad, first of all, don't tell me not to bring beauty and the beast with me. You know how I feel about unfamiliar pla..."

"Mrs. King, are you dressed and ready to meet your husband for dinner?"

"Yes, Husband."

"Come on then, baby."

I hang up the phone and walk back to the hotel to get my wife back. I step out of the elevator and she turns around. Damn, she's beautiful. I reach my hand out and she grabs it to enter the elevator to join me. She has no idea what I have planned for her.

COULDN'T WE BE HAPPILY EVER AFTER

When I wake up, I see a note and a sunflower from my baby. I sit up and go shower. These last few months have been so stressful, and I feel like I'm getting closer to figuring out what happened to Mom. I had been through half of her book trying to connect the dots. She's been in the dreams heavily and I know it's a sign. We still have Kupp on lockdown until he gives us all the information that we need. It's only a matter of time before he cracks and hopefully, that will give us our missing pieces.

A thousand things are going through my mind. I finish my shower and look for the clothes Shad left for me in the closet. I look in the closet and this man has left me a rose gold dress and a white dress. What in the world? Rose gold is my favorite color, but I look damn good in white. Hmmm...I think I'm going to go in white, it looks kind of wedding dress-ish. It's cute though. I shrug my shoulders and slide it on along with the rose gold stilettos he left me. I wet my hair, so it curled up and threw some makeup on. I checked my League phone to see if I had any assignments.

There wasn't an updated blackout list for the week so I guess I could relax. I had a few more people to interview about Mom's missions, including Mrs. Robyn Hodge. She always managed Mom's blackout list and was her eyes and ears, but she kind of disappeared when Mom did. None of us had ever met her, but Mom kept a list of people she encountered. She kept it in her notebook to be sure it was never on a server that could be discovered by hackers or anyone else.

I'm not even sure The League knew about this book, but I am sure they knew about the whereabouts of Mrs. Hodge, and they have been very hush-hush about it. Here goes Shad calling my phone to make sure I was dressed and ready for our dinner date. I'm only on time for missions and flights, so people have to call me to make sure I'm on schedule.

I hang up with him, grab my .22, and walk to the elevator to wait on my man. Shit, it's always better to be caught with it than to be caught without it. Let me call and check on my sister. It goes straight to voicemail. Where the hell is this child? Then I call Grandma J and no answer. What the hell? The elevator dinged and there he was, the love of my life. He grabbed my hand and I walked into the elevator with him.

"Well, damn! You clean up well...I see we're doing the matching thing, huh."

"Shit, why not? It's a special day. You picked the white, I see."

183

"Well, you know I don't shy away from white unless I'm tipsy. Then you know I can get a little clumsy."

"Oh, do I know? We have plenty of time for you to get clumsy all over me."

"Alright now, don't threaten me with a good time."

"Now, if you would just put this blindfold on for me." He twirled me around and put the blindfold on.

"Rashad, you knowwww I don't do blindfolds."

He put his finger over my lips, and I took a deep breath as he put the blindfold on. He guides me off the elevator and he ask me to wait where I am. Then I hear a familiar voice begin to sing, "Guess what I did today, those were the words I said to you, it was last May, don't know the exact day, in my hand, there was a ring..." I know Case when I hear him. I snatch off the blindfold and see our families and friends smiling at me. Rashad was at the end of the aisle with the biggest smile on his face as Case sang Happily Ever After.

Pops stood next to me and held my hand. Then Shunny came up in a rose gold bridesmaid dress to hand me a bouquet.

"What are you up to? What is all of this?"

"Well sis, you didn't get to have a wedding the first time yall got married so you're damn sure going to have one now."

"Oh my god, this is beautiful, you guys! Which one of y'all been on my Pinterest?"

Before I knew it my friends were lining up at the altar in bridesmaids' dresses and Rashad's boys and parents were coming out, too. Dre was there too, surprisingly.

"I guess we're really doing this, huh?"

"Yes, we are baby girl, now come on let's get you to your husband."

I smile at Shunny as she walks down the aisle in front of me and Pops. My palms are sweating like I hadn't already married this man before. Grandma J is smiling from ear to ear as I near the top of the aisle. How in the world did he get her to be the officiant?

"Oh, Grandma J, you and Shunny are tricky ones. I was wondering why I couldn't reach anyone."

"We couldn't tip your nosey ass off, Soli."

"Grandmaaaa? Nosey? Me?"

"Yes you, my beautiful girl. Now, who gives this woman to this man?"

"*WE DO!*" Everyone shouts and Pops steps back so I can join Rashad.

"Alright now! I heard that!"
I look over at him and he smiles.

"Baby, you did all of this for us?"

"Absolutely honey, I would do anything for us."

"Thank you, this was greater than I ever would've planned."

"I know what you like."

"Yes, you do."

"Solice Waytes King, I have loved you since the moment you seduced me in college," everyone bursts out laughing.

"You've had me in a choke hold ever since then."
"LITERALLY," Shunny blurts out.

"Okay Thing 1 and Thing 2 with the jokes"

185

"Alright. Alright, baby. You have played such a major part in me becoming the man that I am today. Through break ups, make ups, surprise engagements and weddings, I never stopped loving you. You feel like home to me because you're my heart in human form. I have experienced pure love by loving you, and I want to continue loving you until there isn't any more breath in my body. Thank you for agreeing to be my wife again."

"Ooo weeee baby, I don't know how I'm going to top that. Oh my gosh, Rashad King. You, my love, are the most selfless and loving person I know. You are my heaven on earth, and I will move mountains to make sure you are safe and happy. I promise to make sure I am intentional in everything I do for and with you. Real love doesn't come knocking every day and luckily you came knocking for me twice. I respect you. I am forever grateful for your love, patience, and understanding. I really have to pinch myself because all this feels like an out of body experience. Man, I love you and I will never let you go again."

"Well, there is nothing else to say but...you may now kiss your bride."

We kiss and everyone cheers.

My love, my heart, my husband, is so thoughtful. I never would've thought in a million years he could plan a whole engagement slash wedding all by himself. I was standing at the altar with my family and friends present. We are happy and free in this moment. I feel everything that I felt the first time we got married and then some. The only person missing was Mom. We lit paper lanterns for her at the end of our ceremony. I'm so grateful that he takes care of my heart.

All I can do is smile because he was right. I look around to see all the love that surrounds us. I also knew with our renewed love and marriage, I would have to be honest this time around. My honesty is the only thing that would keep him safe, not me pushing him away. How do I tell him? I look into his eyes as we have our first dance as husband and wife again.

I know he can see straight through me, but he doesn't ask what's wrong for the sake of enjoying our moment. He pulls me close, and I bury my face in his chest. He lifts my face and kisses my lips. Then he smiles at me and makes us sway to the music. It was like he was rocking my anxiety and struggles away. Mrs. Rebecca pulls me to the side to chat.

"Solice, you know I love you, but I love my baby more. Please take care of my baby's heart. He loves you very much."

"I know, Mrs. Rebecca and I love your baby. I will protect his heart."

"Okay good. Now come on let's get on this dance floor and cut a rug. Maybe Clint will get up with us."

"Alright now! Two of my favorite girls!" Mr. Clint hops up and starts to dance behind Mrs. Rebecca. Pops slides on over to finally get his Daddy-Daughter dance.

"Hi Pops," I smile up at him like I was a little girl all over again when we used to dance with my feet on his.

"Hey baby girl," he kisses me on my forehead.

187

"I'm proud of you both for finding your ways back to each other. True love never dies but it does multiply. I just hope this time around you can talk to one another and most importantly listen. He is the closest person to you and should know everything."

He stops and gives me that parent look. That look you used to get as a kid that says I'm not playing with you.

"Yes sir," I nod, and we keep dancing.

"I'm counting on you Soli. Make me and your mama proud," he spins me around.

"Talk about even the hard things that you cannot always find the words for. That's how me and mama stayed together for so long."

"I know Pops. I will talk to him." I lay my head on his shoulder.

Pops knows a lot more than what he says.

By the end of our special day, we are exhausted and head to the room. I think about a thousand ways to tell him about my other life, but I just need more time. He holds me from behind as I unlock the door and walk inside. Maybe I will talk to Pops about it or Uncle Jack. They had to know something about what Mom was doing. Especially Uncle Jack. They were the cuckoo crew. I need advice on how to make things work with Shad. I tried to hide everything and do everything on my own last time, and it didn't work.

There he is. My husband. He smiles at me and comes over to help me out of my clothes then goes to run our bath. He could tell that I was tense. I go light some candles and pour us a glass of wine.

"Come on babe," he held out his hand for me to get in the tub with him.

"You're amazing. You know that right?"

"Haha, I am. But you made me this way. You've always told me our love can conquer anything and I truly believe that."

"Thank you for believing in us. None of this is possible without you. This is the best I have felt in a long time," I kissed his hand and sunk back into him. He felt like home, and I felt safe. Something was different about Shad.

It was this overwhelming feeling of protection, and he looked like he was getting cut. He was always built but it seems like he had been training. He had matured more during those years we weren't together. Maybe I could trust him to have my back if it came down to some wild League shoot-out shit. I should test him out on the gun range while we're here.

For the rest of the week, he spoiled me rotten. We did everything from ziplining to skydiving. Just two crazy kids back in love. This trip made me forget about everything I had going on at home. I smiled so much my jaw was beginning to hurt.

THE SKY IS FALLING

Shad and I have returned home from our whirlwind, engagement-wedding-honeymoon. It had been a beautiful week for us, but unfortunately, it was time for me to get back to work. Kupp had been ratting out people left and right in hopes of saving his own ass. He still was acting clueless about my Mom's murder. He did give us hella intel on Nelson and he was going to be next on the list after we are done with Liam. Somebody is lying. Either it's him or the higher-ups in The League.

This hit in particular has been difficult to pull off. It's always hard for me to get stuff done in D.C. just for the simple fact that cameras are everywhere, and technology is very advanced with all of the agencies here. They have been on high alert since we took Kupp. But we had a job to do. This Russian real estate investor, Viktor Liam, has purchased several private prisons in the U.S. and has a handful of senators and judges on his payroll. Kupp gave him up in exchange for living a little longer.

One thing I do know, he is tight with Liam and they target high crime areas which are typically black and brown communities. Knowing that they get paid per body, it only makes sense that they would heavily police our communities and give them trumped-up charges and longer sentences.

He is flying in on a private jet in five hours and we have to be on point for everything. Shunny and Emerson have been working on tapping into technology for the last two weeks. Finally, they had a breakthrough two days ago. We have been sleepless ever since they had their breakthrough. We have to finish our planning and it was going to take hella time. Luckily Shad has been busy with a project in Delaware and didn't notice how absent I have been.

Uncle Jack got our automatic sensory weapons set up in all positions where we didn't have enough coverage. As soon as they pick up Liam in their sights, Uncle Jack will be alerted and all he has to do is press fire from his phone. I got the site plans for the Embassy of Russia so I could figure out where and how to enter the building.

Grandma J made me a suit that made it hard for me to be detected by cameras and thermal infrared devices. I tested it with the equipment we had but you can never be too sure with government equipment, so it was best to have the suit and control of their cameras in the area. The unfortunate part is I would have to choose this suit over my normal armored suit. I have to be extra careful. I can't explain any injuries to Rashad because Pops has canceled classes.

We look at the clock and notice that we have two hours left before he is arriving at the Embassy. Tob is walking through the area and releasing his beetle drones. Security in the area is mad high so unfortunately, we are going to have to fight from the knees with this operation.

"Tob, did you send the live feed to Shunny and Emerson yet?"

"All done, Cuz!"

"Sis, it looks like you're going to have to go in underground or over their heads real stealthy."

"Shunny, both of those options sound like shit. You know my sinuses have been all tore up. I hate the smell of everything."

"Don't shoot the messenger, killah. Those are the options with less probability of you being seen. We have the equipment for them not to register your body heat either way. Unfortunately, your overhead method will require you to hang glide."

"Oshun, where in the hell am I supposed to hang glide from?"

"I'm glad you asked, grasshopper. There is a church tower not too far away from the building, maybe 5 blocks."

"5 Blocks?!" I echo in disgust.

"Shunny..."

"You are a professional! 5 Blocks is nothing to you. But you will have to shoot a couple of people on the roof while you hang glide down."

"Shunny, stop messing with your sister. Soli, I have a Russian partner from the war who hates this bastard, and he has us on the inside as the clean-up crew." "Thanks, Uncle Jack. SHUNNY, you play too much. Shit, I'm good but I don't know if I'm that damn good!"

"Soli, come with me so we can get dressed. Keep your stealth suit on under the janitor's outfit and don't look so clean."

I look at Uncle Jack like he is crazy.

"Hello?! Don't look so clean?" Reluctantly, I follow behind him to go get dressed. I have a bad feeling about this. I am feeling queasy.

"Soli, what the hell is wrong with you?"

"Something doesn't feel right, Unc." My stomach was in knots, and I was sweating horribly.

"It's too late for doubt Solice. We have to get this done tonight."

"I know. I know. It might just be my nerves."

"Breathe and let's do this."

I put on my uniform and then we leave to go to the Embassy. When we get into the Embassy, no one paid us any attention because we looked like janitors. Plus, we're black!

"Liam is on his way to the front door. Be prepared." Shunny radios in.

As soon as I turn the corner, the lights went out and shots started flying. *What the fuck!?* I pull my automatic shotgun out of the trash can and began shooting. I activated my night vision glasses to make sure I didn't shoot Unc and kept shooting. Luckily his suit was made with special heat indicators that only we could see with our glasses. I take cover.

"Unc, where are you!?"

"I'm on the second floor, Soli! Get up here now so we can get out. This was a setup! I'm going to kill that son of a bitch Ivan!"

Fuck! I slide down between some columns near the elevator.

"Shunny, send the floor plan to my glasses so I can see where the stairs are located!"

She sends the floor plan and shows me my current location. I would have to run to get down the hall to the stairwell. I check my clip and cock my gun.

"Soli, I'm going out of the first office on the left's window. I will get you from there. I have already cleared a path."

"10-4 Unc, I'm making a break for it!" I get up and run down the hall. When I turn around to check my back. *Pat. Pat. Pat.* Bullets are flying. Shit! I'm hit. A random chick in black is shooting at me. She shot me in the shoulder and leg. I put my back to the door of the stairwell and began shooting back. I hit her in the side. I shove myself backwards through the door, watching my front and my back as I'm going up the steps to the second floor. I finally make it to the office Unc was talking about. I kick the door open and go hide behind a long curtain by the window.

Got dammit! I cannot believe I got caught up in another assassin's hit. How in the hell did The League not have the specs? Why were there multiple hits on this fool? Who the hell did he piss off to have two hits on him?

"Shunny, can you hear me?"

"Yea, Sis, I can hear you. What the hell is going on in...."

"I'm hit, and I gotta get out of here and fast!" My breaths are shaky, and my adrenaline is the only thing keeping me from passing out.

"Okay, I see your location, I just need you to get outside on the ledge. Is it safe for you to move?"

"No, I can still hear them running through the halls. Is Uncle Jack still on the other roof?"
The footsteps and voices are getting closer to the office.

"Wait one sec, let me get him on the earpiece. Uncle Jack, what's your locale?"

"10-4 Shunny, Uncle Jack checking in and I've got eyes on Soli." I could tell Unc was about to start bugging out.

"Soli, can you hear Uncle Jack?!" Shunny was frantic and talking fast.

"Yes, I can hear him. Uncle Jack, do you have a visual on opposing targets?" They open the office door.
"I have a visual, and I'll clear you a path in 5...4...3...2...1!"

Swoosh. Swoosh. Swoosh.

The bullets flew right past me and hit the targets and I got up and ran for my life. There was no way I could die here. I had just restarted my life with Rashad, and I

195

wasn't going to lose him again. I saw the zip line to the building that Uncle Jack was at and connected myself.

"Hey! You stop where you are, or I'll shoot!"

"SOLI! DUCK!", yelled Uncle Jack and all I could do was cover my head and slide down the zipline. Gunfire was everywhere and by the grace of my Creator and ancestors I made it to the other side and Unc pulled me up.

"Shit, Soli, don't ever scare me like that again!" I just lay there gasping for air, until the pain from my earlier wounds kicked in.

"We gotta get you to a hospital, Soli. I will meet you both in the back alley."

Once Uncle Jack helped me down the fire escape and into the SUV, I cried. Shunny put pressure on my gunshots wounds.

"Sis, why are you crying?"

"I can't keep doing this shit yall. What if this is how Mom got killed? Who's to say that this wasn't a setup?"

"Soli, it might have been a coincidence, but someone has to answer for the confusion. Senator Marks had his hand in everything from trafficking to paying off judges to give Black people longer sentences and getting kickbacks from the state for the number of prisoners coming in and doing free labor."

"Or, maybe she's right, Shunny, we cannot be so naïve to believe The League didn't know about the double hit." There were so many questions and I know once Shad saw me like this, he would have so many more. I called

Shad and told him to meet us at the BridgePoint Capitol Hill Hospital.

I took off all of my gear and equipment before we got to the hospital. I had to make sure I had one of my fake IDs so they couldn't easily place me at the hospital. This night just did not add up to me at all. Good thing I pulled Sara before this assignment. My spirit had been bothering me and Mom had been visiting me in my dreams.

"We're going to say that we found you shot on the sidewalk and that someone shot you during a robbery, got it?"

"Okay, Unc."

"Alright let's do this! Look alive because you never know where the enemy may lie or if they followed us. Shunny, are you strapped?"

"Always."

"SOMEONE HELP! Me and my daughter found this young lady on the street, and she's been shot!" The ER nurses ran up to me and lifted me on a stretcher then took me to the back.

"Ma'am, can you tell us what happened?"

"I was walking out of my apartment and some random person just told me to hand over my purse and I refused then he shot me in the leg and shoulder."

"It's okay honey, we're going to take real good care of you."

I knew I could only stay long enough for them to treat my wound and be out. I ended up passing out from the blood loss. When I came through, there was my baby pacing the floor. I could tell he was confused and anxious.

"Baby." I reached my hand out to him.

"Soli, please don't ever scare me like this again." He rushes to my side and kisses my forehead.

"What the hell happened, Solice?"

"Baby, we can't talk about it here."

"What?! You're in the hospital with gunshot wounds in your leg and shoulder. And you don't want to…." The Doctor walks in.

"Hello, Mrs. Randall. I assume you're Mr. Randall?" said the doctor as he looked at the both of us. Rashad immediately gave me the "What the fuck?" look and nodded his head yes to the doctor.

"So, your wounds are not life-threatening. They are easy to treat since the bullets passed through. Yay for that, but I do have some other news concerning your current condition."

"Other news? Other news like what?"

"Well Mrs. Randall, you were extremely lucky that your blood loss did not impact your pregnancy and the baby is perfectly fine. We're going to do an ultrasound to see how far along you are. Your blood pressure is quite elevated, so I do recommend hubby takes you home and lets you get some rest. Other than that, we have removed the bullet and stitched you up. Have a great day, guys. The ultrasound tech will be in shortly" The doctor exits out of the room and there I sat in confusion, speechless. Truthfully, I am horrified.

"What did he just say?", asks Shad as he stares at me. I couldn't respond. I didn't know what to say or do but cry. Uncle Jack and Shunny walked in shortly after the doctor walked out.

"Solice, why the hell are you crying again?" Uncle Jack was confused and hated a whole bunch of crying.

"She's pregnant Unc. And I need somebody to tell me what the hell is going on around here. Solice, you promised me there would be no more secrets once we got married again.

"PREGNANT?", both Unc and Shunny blurted out together.

"Soli you picked a damn good time to get pregnant. I knew this shit was going to happen. I need a cigar. Come on let's get the hell out of here." Unc tossed my duffle bag on the floor and told Rashad to get me dressed and out of the hospital in the next 20 minutes. He and Shunny left out and went back to the SUV. The ultrasound tech came in and starts the ultrasound as I lay on the table. After a few seconds, the heartbeat came over the monitor.

"Congratulations looks like you're about 7 weeks pregnant. You should schedule an appointment with your OBG-YN soon," she walks out of the room.

Me and Shad stay silent the whole time he is getting me dressed. I know he is angry with me. Most of all he probably was hurt. While the nurses are busy, he helps me outside to his car and drives out of the parking garage with Shunny and Unc behind him. This ride felt like an eternity. My stomach turns with the closer we get to my parents' house. I feel him grab my hand as I stare out of the window. We pull up at my parents' house in Maryland, which is safe for us. I wanted to be far away from D.C. as possible at this point. We sat in the driveway, and I knew I had to explain to my entire family what the hell was going on.

We all got out of the vehicles and head inside. Grandma J was already here. She and Pops were waiting for us.

"Mama J told me what happened already."

"Pops I..."

"Soli, you must think your Pops was naïve when it came to your mama? I knew when she was in some deep shit. You know why? Because she told me, especially when it was going to impact our family. What makes you think I don't know what type of mess my daughters are in? At the very least you need to allow my son-in-law to be a rock for you like I was for your mama. No, she didn't tell me every single detail about her assignments, but I knew I loved and married one of the most dangerous women in the world. But I also knew that she wanted to change the world and that there were rules to that change. I told you at the wedding that you two needed to talk."

"You wanna tell your daddy one more thing he doesn't know?" I looked at Grandma J like she had two heads when she said that.

"Tell me what Mama J?"

"She's pregnant" before I could even get it out, Shad answers for me.

"H-H-H-ow did you know?"

"Grandma J knows everything baby, plus your mother told me in a dream."

Is this the reason why I kept seeing her in my dreams? She was always cradling a child and saying, "It's time to leave my love and takes the baby away with her." Was she telling me it was time for me to leave The League because I had something more precious to protect? A single tear fell from my eyes as everyone began to hug me.

"Go talk to your husband baby.", said Grandma J as she places my hand inside Shad's.

I walk behind Shad as he guides me to the garden. I could tell he was still processing everything.

"Baby, I'm sorry I didn't know I was preg…"

"Soli, I already know what's going on with you but you gotta stop. Whatever it is that you're working on right now, you gotta stop. You are carrying our child, and I couldn't bare if something happened to either one of you. I'm not naïve either, but I need you to tell me what is going on so I can protect our family. Dre gave me a file on you thicker than Serena." *What the fuck?* Dre gave him a file on me?

"There's no easy way I can say this." I turn to look him in the eyes.

"Baby, umm, I'm an assassin and I have been one since we met. My first mission was an Aruba trip during spring break before we met. Traveling the world as the operations and logistics manager is my cover job. Grandma J, Shunny, and Uncle Jack, all help me in the completion of my assignments.

"Wow, so when I asked you if you were a killer, you really were. I don't know why you didn't think you could rely on me Soli" He scoffs and got up to go for a walk. I just sat there, because what else could I do to hurt my husband?

After about 30 minutes he returns and stares at me. He grabs both of my hands and pulls me up.

"Solice, I love you more than anything in this world, but…"

"But you can't do this?"

"No, that's not what I was going to say. I was going to say but, I can't have you out here fighting and shooting while you are pregnant. What do you need to do to stop being an assassin?"

"Well baby, you just don't stop. There are rules to this. My only way out is to bring someone else in. I don't even have any prospects in training so…"

"I'll do whatever it takes. Pops and Uncle Jack have already started training me in martial arts and gunplay. Pops started training me while we were separated, right after Dre gave me the file. I have been practicing on the days I go to the gym. Uncle Jack lets me come to the range and shoot whatever."

"Rashad, I have killed people. Can you do that without letting it eat away at you? Baby your heart is so pure. I never wanted that for you. You are the only thing in my life that hadn't been touched by this side of me."

"Solice when I told you that I will protect you and our children by any means necessary I meant that. It's either us or them and I'm not living without y'all. I know what you are into. I have known for a while now, I just wanted you to trust me enough to let me know. Dre had suspicions and he told me without telling the CIA. I decided to remarry you despite knowing that you aren't perfect, and you had secrets that you weren't ready to tell me about."

I couldn't even be mad that he had been training to protect me. Protect us. I just wish he would've found out from me. That was my bad. I am glad that Pops and Uncle Jack took him under their wings and trained him safely.

"If Dre figured it out there's no telling who else knows. I haven't been sloppy so I don't understand how he could figure it out."

"Baby, you've been taking out some of the same people he's been assigned to watch or set up."

"Is he a double agent?"

"Possibly, unlike you, he can't tell me everything about his life and I don't expect him to. Pops even gave me insight on how he and Mom handle this process in their marriage, and we can do the same."

"Well, what do I tell The League?"

"First, you tell them you're pregnant. I'm sure your mother and Grandma J have both gone through this. Women getting pregnant isn't some phenomenon, so there has to be some type of structure involved."

"You're right. I will talk to Grandma J to see how we should proceed. She's the OG so she should know how to handle The League and get me out of combat."

"Or get me into combat."

"Baby, I don't you getting hurt either."

"We're a team, Lice."

Uncle Jack came from inside the house with a worried look on his face.

"Hey, uhh you guys should see this."

"What is it, Unc?"

"Shunny was able to pull footage of who shot you" Unc pulled out the pictures and I couldn't believe who it was. Me and Shad look at each other.

"Kayla?!"

This bitch hadn't been on our radar in so long, I had completely forgotten about her. Why in the hell would she be at the Embassy of Russia? Before I could start asking questions out loud, Shunny started with her specs. "I'm sure we're all wondering why Kayla was at the Embassy of Russia. I ran her face through our facial recognition system. I don't know why we didn't do this while she was dating bro in law. It turns out that Kaylana Desiree Moss was a military brat, her dad was a Navy Seal, looks like her mother was born and raised in Germany. Appears mom had a history as a prostitute.

Dad bounced on her and her mom once she was born and his deployment was over to return to his wife who also welcomed a baby boy two months before Kayla's birth. Also, it looks like Kayla lived a pretty hard-knock life in Germany since she had a sprinkle of melanin. She has similar training to yours in combat. She became a foreign exchange student in her junior year of high school and resided in California. Coincidently, the same year she came to the States, her father died in a freak accident. After obtaining U.S. citizenship, she attended ULA and majored in Architectural Studies. I assume that's how you met her, Shad."

I look at my husband and he is pale in disbelief. I could tell he is sick to his stomach.

"Andddd...there is more. The League has her on the red list." Shunny looks over at us, shaking her head.

"You can't be fucking serious! AND THEY DIDN'T THINK TO WARN ME?" I was in total disbelief.

"Baby, I had been getting strange calls and being followed for the last few months, but I didn't want to scare you. Not even scare you but enrage you."

"Shad, you mean to tell me this girl has been stalking you like prey and NOW she's trying to kill me? I'm going to wipe her off the face of the earth. No ifs, ands, or buts. It's on!"

The red list was a list of assassins to be aware of. Since they didn't make it to the blacklist, we typically let lower-level assassins keep watch on them. How could The League let her fall through the cracks and just who in the hell is she working for? I was on someone's list.

"There's more, sis. She graduated from ULA the same time you graduated from Bowie. She moved to D.C. shortly afterwards. Appears you got on her list when you started taking out some government officials that interfered with some Russian business. Looks like infiltration is what she gets off on and probably how she got so close to Shad. But it also looks like she really liked Shad based on her socials. He's still posted on her pages. And if I do a quick scan of Shad's socials it looks like old girl has still been stalking his pages, using different VPNs.

So, this chick is going to be a problem until we take her out."

"Solice, it's time we call the head."

I look over at Grandma J. I am scared as hell. She walks into the house and grabs her burner phone.

"Ehhh, Pop it's time. Ya Bussa-Bussa and get the job done.

"How you mean?"

"They messed with da bebe. Put 'em in the dead house."

"Yuh gawh be kiddin. Me on the way. Trouble don't set up like the rain," Poppy hangs up the phone. Shad looks at me confused as hell.

"Who is she talking to?"

"Poppy."

"Poppy? Your grandfather?!"

"Yep, all hell is about to break loose."

Even Uncle Jack looks spooked. If Poppy was called that means The League's higher-ups have some explaining to do. I look over at Pops and he's silent. He already knows that Poppy is crazy, and Grandma J calls him when shit goes south.

"Poppy will be here in a few hours. He wants everyone to stay here tonight. Jack, you'll be picking Poppy up from the airport," he nods and goes into the house.

I hadn't seen Poppy since Mom's memorial service. As grown as I was, I am still scared of him, even though I loved him to death. He is built like John Henry even at the age of 75. He doesn't talk much but he never had to say much because his presence precedes him. Anybody who's anyone knows, don't mess with his family. Shad had only met Poppy twice, but he even knew Poppy was not to be played with. Knowing that he was moving that fast to get here, when he normally takes his time, shows that he was beyond pissed. All of his grands are bebe to him no matter the age. He was just like any other grandparent. He was going to ride for his grands.

One thing we had to do in the meantime was find out all the information we could about Kayla before he arrived.

"Are you able to see if she has a bingo list or a hit book stored on any servers?" I ask Shunny.

"I will try my best. Unc calls into The League and sees why she was there while Soli was there and who she works for."

"10-4, going to make the call now. I'm sure they've caught wind of what happened tonight anyway." Unc walks out to go make a call. That call didn't take long because Shunny's phone starts going crazy with all types of info on Kayla. Uncle Jack gets into his car and leaves afterwards.

"Sis you should see this."

"What else could it be Shunny?"

I grab her phone and scroll through the rest of the information about Kayla. I drop the phone on the floor.

"Shit, it turns out the next hit is me. A-A-And Mom's name was on her list too. Could she have...? There's no way in hell. Either she was trying to kill me for Shad or kill me to finish Fuentes' dirty work. She is

Fuentes's secret pitbull. Fuentes's best friend Boris Igor was killed by Mom when she was in the Marines. It looks like he was kidnapping young boys and turning them into soldiers. Mom and team was sent in to rescue the boys and he was killed in the process. Boris Igor had a sister named Inessa Igor. She was a prostitute and had a daughter with an African American Navy Seal. Sound familiar?"

"Kayla is trying to avenge her uncle. I guess she was his first soldier. That's why it is easy for her to fly under the radar, and it looks like she did it by trying to come after you and Mom." Me and Shunny stare at each other. I look back down at her phone.

"It looks to be that way, Sis. Based on these phone pings, she and Fuentes were in contact with one another the day Mom disappeared. The pings also showed her in the area where the accident happened." This shit is unreal. My heart starts hurting. I start to hyperventilate and everything around me starts spinning. I black out.

"Baby Girl, wake up. Can you hear me?"
Everything around me is blurry and all I see are shadows and shapes.

"Baby girl, I need you to sit up."
This had to be a dream because there was no way I am pregnant and hearing this voice. I sit up and rub my eyes.

"Poppy?"

"Yes, Bebe. Me here." He rubs my cheek.
Then I feel this smaller hand grab mines. The smell was familiar. A smell I hadn't smelt in a long time.

"Mommy?"

I began to shake uncontrollably. She moves my hand to her face and nods.

"Am I dead? T-T-This cannot be real? I can't be dead because Poppy is here."

"I will explain later but we've got to go. They're looking for you."

"Where, where is Pops? Where is Rashad and Shunny? Do they know?"

"Baby, you ask too many questions. Only Pops, Poppy and Grandma J knew. Now let's go. Rashad has Mina and we're taking you to Barbados."

Taking me to Barbados? What the fuck is going on?

Made in the USA
Middletown, DE
05 January 2024